I read' Thistown to two of my children. All three of us were gripped by it. Malcolm McKay creates a compelling new world of the familiar and the strange, and weaves a spell for the reader that makes it an addictive read "Original, fresh, funny and inventive…highly recommended"

Juliet Stevenson.

CHILDREN'S REVIEWS FOR THISTOWN

Wonderful. Each chapter left you in suspense. One of the reasons why it is so magnificent is that it has a completely different storyline. There was no part I didn't like. Each character has his own specific personality.....

FINN B. 10.

What I particularly enjoyed about THISTOWN was the emphasis on true friendship. The book teaches many morals, standing up for what you believe in, and the importance of loyalty and perseverance and ultimately that those in the wrong will be the ones to fail.

MOLLY PECK, 12.

I really like the book. I think it is great for people of my age. It is fun to read and also exciting. The part I like most is the end where they end up going to the cornfields....

LEAH BROWN, 13.

I thoroughly enjoyed reading THISTOWN as it is very different from anything I have read before. It was like THISTOWN had some kind of gravitational pull because i could not put it down. I was on tenterhooks all through and my heart was racing when Alice jumped in the sun cone. The ending was very surprising...

DANIELLE WOODFORD, 12.

I read it in a day. Nothing could tear me away from this book. Never have I seen dictatorship portrayed as clearly as in Thistown.

REBECCA BOWEN, 13,

THISTOWN

Malcolm Mckay

For Alice

<u>Malcolm McKay</u>

Malcolm McKay has been writing novels and for the theatre and television for over thirty years. His work for young people includes: *The Amazing Adventures of Spaceman Jack Fitton* which toured schools for many years.

More recently, he has been writer/director of many successful television films including the awardwinning *A Wanted Man* trilogy, *Redemption* and an adaptation of Emile Zola's *La Bête Humaine*. He has also adapted the BBC serial *Gormenghast* and wrote the police series *NCS Manhunt*.

He has three novels published, *The Lack Brothers* (Transworld), *Breaking Up* (Pegasus) and *The Path* (Baseline).

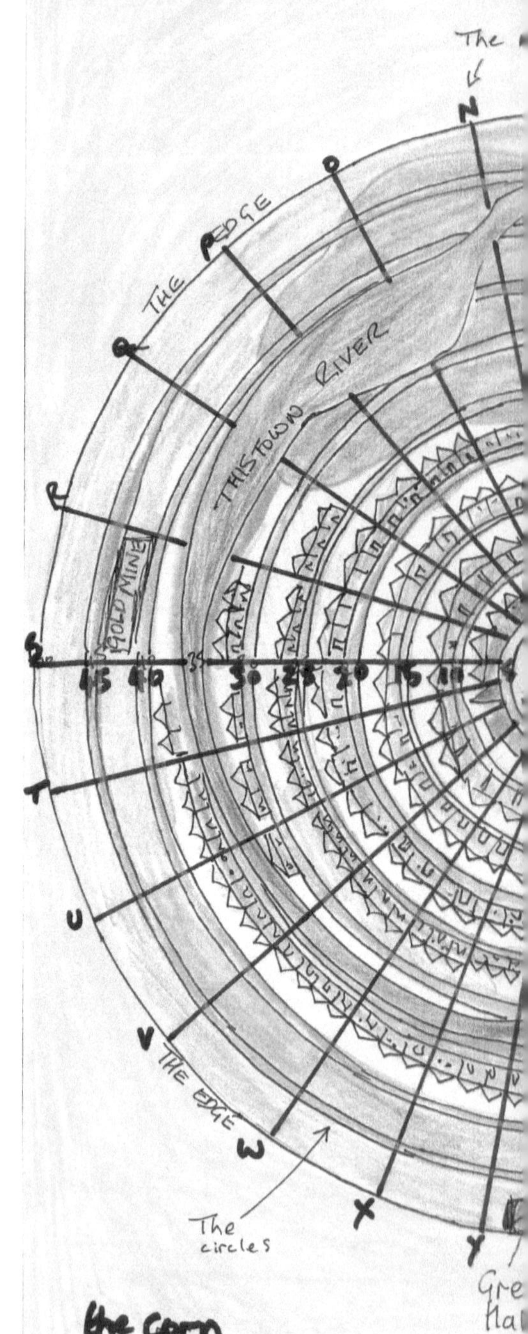
the corn
The
N
P
THE P EDGE
THE EDGE
Q
THISTOWN RIVER
R
GOLD MINE
S 45 40 35 30 25 20 15 10
T
U
V
THE EDGE
W
X
Y
The
circles
Gre
Hal

the corn

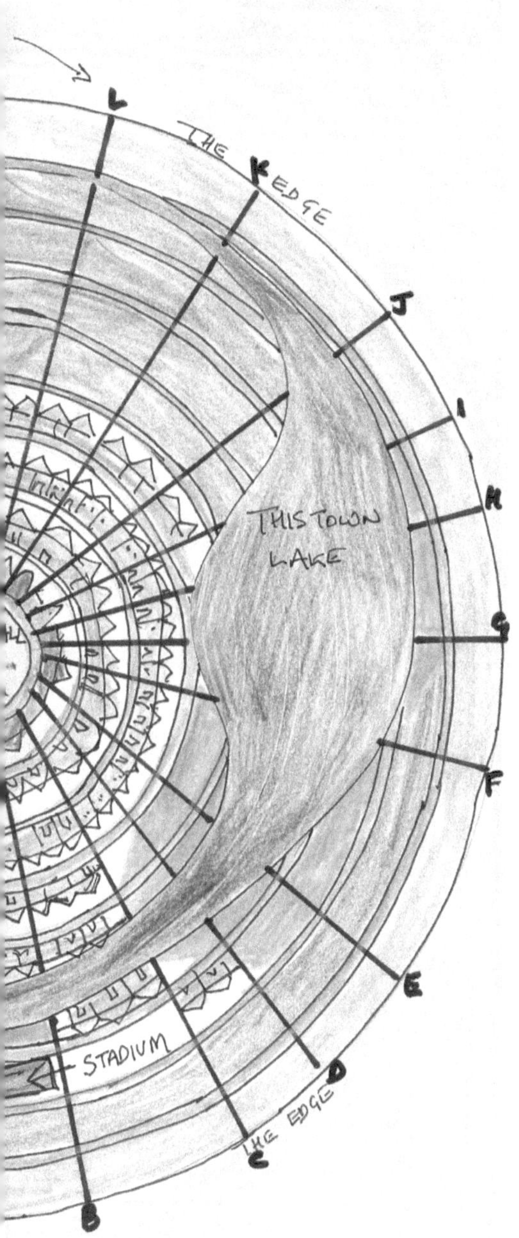

thistown

A TOWN IN CIRCLES

Somewhere beyond the rain, the wind and the stars, and as far from Earth as it 's possible to be, there was a town so old that no-one can remember how or when it began. It was called Thistown, the town where time stood still. There are some who believe that it was the very first town ever. But whenever it started, there is one thing for certain, it hadn't changed at all since that time. It seemed to every Thistonian that their town had always been exactly as it was; the same houses, the same avenues, the same Green, and the same Town hall, all stretching back in time forever. And of course all the same people too, the twenty-three thousand Thistonians, who knew each other for as long as memory can be.

Thistown was called Thistown because no-one had ever been outside it, pointed back and said, 'That town.' It is very important to remember that. No-one had ever left Thistown. *No-one, ever.* They'd never left because the town was surrounded by the cornfields that stretched as far as the eye could see, and if you went into them you disappeared. Or bits of you would disappear, and you ended up like Ron Rasper from Avenue A who put one foot into the corn and spent the rest of his days stomping around on an iron leg. So if there was a world on the other side of the corn the Thistonians didn't know about it, and couldn't even imagine it. The corn made sure they stayed where they were.

Thistown was built in circles. The inner circle was called the Green and on it were hundreds of oak trees with dark broad trunks and great blue-black swarms of bluebirds fluttering around them. They were friendly birds, but lately they'd begun to peck and shriek. It's because of what Belle fell over and made Thistown change forever.

The rest of the town was like a giant catherine wheel with each circle being surrounded by another circle. Around the Green was the First Circle. All along this were the stores, the police station, the stables, and on the top end, the Town Hall, all facing onto the Green. Outside the First Circle came, logically enough, the second circle, and along this were the workshops and factories of Workshop Way, with great dray donkeys dragging heavy loads from one huge building to the next. Outside Workshop Way were forty-eight other circles, each bigger than the last. A long way out from the Green, between Circles Thirty-five and Forty-five there were mainly fields of cereals and vegetables, or woods, or pretty orchards. And here were also the ancient silver and gold mines which were boarded up now as everyone already had all the jewellery they needed. The last, or outermost circle of all was the Fiftieth, also know as the Edge which is where the town stopped and the cornfields began.

Running from the Green in the middle of Thistown to the Edge on the outside were twenty-five Avenues. They ran straight like the spokes of a wheel and each was named after a letter, from A to Y. So apart from a few pokey alleys and crooked lanes, it was very easy to get around Thistown. All you said was something like Avenue X on the Twenty-second Circle and everyone knew immediately where you were.

Alice Bright came out of her house on on the Seventh Circle, turned left on Avenue W and walked towards the Town Hall on the Green. Like everyone else Alice had been the same age for as long as anyone could remember. No-one had ever grown older and no-one had ever been younger in Thistown. (And nobody had ever died either. In fact the very words die, or dead, were unknown at this time in Thistown - although this happy state wasn't to last for much longer.)

Alice was twelve years old, had always been twelve and always would be. She was a tall, thin girl who walked with her feet stuck out. She had a round, smiley face, with bright red lips, short blond straight hair, and sparkling blue eyes. You never knew quite where you were with Alice, one minute she was up and laughing and joking with her eyes sparkling and the next minute she was down and scowling and fed up with everybody. Her name should have been Alice Updown.

As she walked down Avenue W she looked back at her tiny house. Everyone had a house of their own, consisting of a bedroom, a kitchen, a living room and a bathroom, which suited everybody fine because nobody lived with anybody else and so they only needed one of everything. And that's what Alice had, which was just fine for her too, thank you.

She sang to herself as she walked along Avenue W towards the Town Hall. She was going to take her place on the Town Assembly. She'd been elected to sit on it only two months before and was still very proud of herself. (Although sometimes a bit unsure of herself too.) Little did she know that her happiness wasn't even going to last until the end of the day.

She was expecting to meet her best friend, Sam. He'd also just been elected to the Assembly and usually walked this way from his house on Avenue R on the Fifth Circle. Today he was a bit late so she sat on a wall, and as she waited she looked away from the Green all the way back along Avenue W to the cornfields on the the Edge. Like everyone else she often wondered about the waving, bright yellow corn. No-one knew how the corn made you disappear, or made bits of you disappear. It was frightening and had always been a mystery. It was, of course, absolutely forbidden to everybody. There were huge signs all round the Edge, reading:

"BEWARE HUNGRY CORN"

"FORBIDDEN ON PAIN OF IMMEDIATE DISAPPEARANCE"

"PUT IN A TOE, LOSE A TOE"

"NO-ONE HAS *EVER* RETURNED FROM THE CORN"

"Alice! Hurry up, we'll be late." It was Sam striding along the Fifth Circle wearing a huge brown coat. He walked straight past her without stopping.

"You telling me?" said Alice leaping off the wall, "I've been waiting for *you!*"

But Sam was already five yards ahead of her. Samson Stead, or Steady Sam, or Big Sam - take your pick - was taller than everybody else who was twelve and had always been twelve etc. In fact some parts of him were so big, his legs for example, that it was never entirely clear if he had full control of all the bits, and so he tended to occasionally fall over his knees or crack his ankles together. Clumsy Sam might have been the best name for him. His hair stuck up around his head and he wore thick round glasses which made his eyes seem as big as the reast of his body. The main point to remember about Sam is that he was sensible. In fact Sensible Sam would have been the best name of all. You could always rely on old Sam.

He turned back as Alice caught him up, "There's an investigation," he said.

"What?" Alice tried to keep up.

"In the Assembly. Something's happened."

"What's happened?"

"It's important."

"What is?"

"Belle fell over."

"What's so important about that?" Alice was having to run to keep up with him. "She's always falling over."

"Not over something like this."

"Something like what?"

"Keep up, Alice."

"I'm trying, Sam. Can you slow down?"

"Nope. We'll be late."

"What did she fall over?" It was no good, Sam was striding away on his huge legs. "Sam!"

She hurried after him. As they passed the Third Circle, she looked over at their old school standing crumbling and empty and just for a second felt nostalgic.

"You remember?"

"Yes, Alice I remember."

"Oh, I forgot, you remember everything, don't you, big brain?"

"I remember the school because you talk about it every time we go past it."

"Well I liked it."

"We haven't been for over a hundred and fifty years."

It was true and also true that Alice could hardly remember going anyway. She could vaguely recollect lessons, but slowly they'd all stopped attending, and their teachers hadn't minded at all. Everyone agreed that they all knew everything they needed to know, so what was the point of going to school forever?

"I still miss it though," she said. "We used to see everybody every day."

"There's Fortuna," said Sam.

By this time they'd come to the Green and coming through the Oaks was Fortuna Mink, the third and last young person who'd been elected to the Assembly. She had a pale yellow skin, a triangular shaped face, and black almond eyes that were as dark as her thick hair which was cut in a square fringe across her forehead. She was dressed in her usual black with a red string bow in her hair. She looked like a cat and mostly sounded like one too with a kind of high, light voice which sometimes fot lost in the wind.

If Alice was honest with herself she would have to admit she didn't like Fortuna too much - she was just too smooth and let's face it, cat like. She would have also liked to talk to Sam about it, but Sam as usual didn't make any judgement on people. (Too sensible for that) If you'd asked him what he thought about Fortuna, he'd have said, "Well, she's ah? She's Fortuna." Thank you, Sam, thought Alice, do you ever notice anything?

"Hi, Sam," said Fortuna, "Alice." Her silky, low voice made it sound like Aliss.

Sam smiled. For some reason when Fortuna spoke everybody listened and seemed to appreciate her, which was probably another reason that Alice didn't like her too much.

"At least there's something worth talking about on the Assembly today," Fortuna said, making assembly sound like assimbly.

"What's worth talking about?" Alice was still hoping to find out what was going on.

"The Sleeping Man, Alice"

"What Sleeping Man?"

But Fortuna had already followed Sam up the great steps (which he took two at a time) and through the huge wooden doors into the Town Hall, leaving Alice following behind and beginning to feel depressed. Why wouldn't anyone talk to her? And what could be so important, or even interesting, about a sleeping man? Everyone slept didn't they?

THE SLEEPING SUBSTANCE

The nurse at the Hospital was called Dorothy Pine. She was a large, bustling, woman with a big chest who was always hot and red in the face. She was the one who had bandaged Belle Fellow's hand after she had fallen over in Duster Alley. Belle probably knew more about Thistown than anyone else because she spent every second walking or running round it and poking her nose into everything. That day she had been her usual stringy, ten year old self, (always been ten.... etc), who generally fell over anything that was in her way. Her real name was Fiona but for a long time - about sixty years or so - she had been nicknamed Dumbelina because she was so clumsy, and as more years had gone by, this had been shortened to Belle. She usually fell over something, or knocked into it, or dropped something else on average three or four times a week. She didn't seem to mind at all. "That's what I am," she said, "Belle Fellows Over. And that's what you're going to have to put up with. Because I'm not going to change, am I?" She didn't seem to mind the blood either, or even occasional broken bones.

Nurse Pine was on the witness bench. She had better things to do than put bandages on Belle (again) and had been impatient with her. That's what she told the Assembly. Alice, Sam, Fortuna and the other seven Assembly members sat on big, worn, red chairs with the stuffing hanging out of them, around a huge old, scratched, wooden table.

Above them Arthur Pen, editor of the Opinion Newspaper leaned forward over the wooden rail in the public gallery to hear better. Ted Thrust, the editor of the Clarion, the town's other newspaper, was sitting next to him. Obviously their reports wouldn't agree, because they never agreed on anything - what's the point of having two newspapers that said the same thing? But that didn't mean they didn't get on. Pen liked Thrust's big walrus moustache, and Thrust liked Pen's bald head and ring of white hair. As Nurse Pine was speaking, Thrust gave Pen a mint from a packet. That was the last thing Ted Thrust ever gave Arthur Pen out of friendship.

"I didn't think about it." said Nurse Pine. "It was just Belle falling over like usual. She's always doing it, ain't she?" She pursed her lips in disapproval. "It was only when I was filling out the report that I asked her, what did you trip over then? For official reasons, see? It's the Hospital Accident Report Form. We have to know."

Percy Pike, the Head of the Assembly, was a thin, awkward man with long thin lips, and a nose like a pointed fish's mouth that stuck out from the middle of his face. He was impatient and pretty snappy. He leant forward and said, "So woman, what *did* Belle fall over in Duster Alley?"

"I'll tell you," said the Nurse with her big chest heaving. "I wrote it in red ink in my Report." She paused for a second to keep everyone waiting a bit longer, then she said, "As far as I know, she fell over a sleeping man."

The members looked at each other across the table. They already knew this much and having a nap was hardly something that needed to be investigated by the Town Assembly, was it? There had to be more to it than that. And there was.

"So?" asked Pike impatiently.

"I told the doctor," said Nurse Pine as if it was the only thing an intelligent nurse could have done.

"Which doctor?" asked Alice, being mischievous. She well knew that Nurse Pine couldn't have been entirely sure which doctor she'd told it to, as the two doctors were identical twins. They lived in two small identical houses next door to one another on Avenue A. They had identical furniture and identical clothes. It was sometimes said that they couldn't tell themselves apart. Like most people in Thistown their original names had been forgotten and they'd been called Stitch and Slice for as long as anyone could remember. Or was it Slice and Stitch? It didn't matter. If you called one, the other would come anyway.

"I don't know which one," said Pine. "All I know is, he was talking to Sergeant Willis at the Hospital door, because Flouncy, that is, the Sergeant, had come in to write an accident report."

"Please will you get on with it." Pike was getting impatient. He had an idea to go fishing up on the Thistown river.

"He said he'd check on on the sleeping man on his way home." The Nurse gave Pike a hurt look.

"Then let's call Sergeant Willis!" said Pike impatiently, wanting to get this ridiculous woman off the witness bench as quickly as possible.

But Nurse Pine didn't get up, she merely moved sideways and was immediately replaced in the centre of the bench by the huge form of Detective Sergeant Flouncy Willis of the Thistown police in his grey and crumpled suit. He was a nice man with a fat face that flopped and folded when he spoke. He was usually very eager to please and he tried to look as efficient as possible as he snapped open the hard cover of his official Thistown police notebook.

He said "At four o'clock yesterday I was in the vicinity of the First Circle Hospital and I was approached by Nurse Pine who asked if I would investigate a sleeping substance in Duster Alley. I agreed to do so and went to Duster Alley where I came immediately upon the subject....."

"Subject? What subject?" asked Croker. He was one of the oldest (and deafest) on the Town Assembly and a little slow on the uptake.

"The subject, being the sleeping man," said Willis, clutching his notebook. "I leaned down and I touched him on the shoulder, like this." He stuck a finger in the air and demonstrated how he had prodded. "There was no response to this, so I shook his shoulder and said...." He opened his notebook again to check the exact wording, "I said, 'Wake up you fellow, this is no place to be lying asleep.'" Willis snapped his notebook shut with a flourish and flopped his big face around a nervous grin.

There was a silence in the hall. Everybody was expecting Willis to say something else. He didn't.

"Then what happened?" asked Sam peering through his glasses. Like Alice, he too, was beginning to wonder what this was all about.

"He wouldn't wake up. Or couldn't," said Willis, beginning to sound a bit less sure of himself. Then he told them that he'd immediately run back to the Hospital and fetched Doctors Stitch and Slice. The three of them with Nurse Pine puffing behind had ran back up Duster Alley. The sleeping substance was exactly where he'd been left. He hadn't moved an inch. Stitch or Slice, put a stethoscope to the Sleeping Man's chest and heard nothing. Slice or Stitch held his wrist for a pulse and could feel nothing. Nurse Pine put a thermometer in his mouth and couldn't read it because she had forgotten her glasses. Sergeant Willis wrote it all down in his notebook. Then they stood back and looked down on the man.

"I suggested we take him immediately back to the Hospital, sir." said Willis to Pike. "And so we procured a cart from Workshop Way and went back with him the way we came."

THE NO-LIFE MAN

Alice leaning forward across the table. She'd perked up and now she wanted to know more.

"Why don't we ask the doctors what they did?" asked Sam.

Willis shuffled sideways towards Nurse Pine as the twin doctors crammed themselves onto the other end of the bench. They wore identical dark green suits. If you glanced quickly you would have sworn you were seeing double.

"We tried to wake him up," said Stitch.

"Did you succeed?" Fortuna asked.

"No,"

"You couldn't wake him up at all?" asked Sam looking puzzled.

"We tried everything," said Slice.

"Everything we knew," said Stitch.

"And everything I knew too," said Nurse Pine as if she knew more than either of them.

"Was there any breathing?" asked Sam.

"No." The twin doctors said it together.

"Did his chest move up and down?" added Pike.

"No."

There was a silence in the huge room.

Finally Sam said what everyone else was thinking, "Well, if he's not moving, if he's not even breathing, that can only mean one thing."

"What thing?" asked Fortuna looking straight at him as if she was daring him to say it.

"No breath, means no life," said Sam simply and shrugged his shoulders.

"No Life? How can someone have no life?" Pike laughed uneasily showing his brown teeth.

Alice was beginning to wonder too. She gave a puzzled look to Sam. Everyone had life, didn't they? She knew that for certain. They'd all been there forever in Thistown. How could someone suddenly have no life? What was going on?

"You mean that he's a No-Life Man?" asked Fortuna.

"A what?" asked Pike. This was already all getting beyond him.

"A No-Life Man." Fortuna said it again. "That's what it is, isn't it?"

This sounded as strange to them as anything ever had. If you'd have said, trees with their roots in the air, or sky falling on your head, or birds that flew in the ground, it would have seemed equally bizarre. A No-Life Man? Nobody had ever heard of such a thing.

"That's impossible," said Alice finally, "How can you have no life?" She looked at Sam. He raised his eyebrows.

"Well, who is he?" said Pike hoping for something he could understand.

"Did you recognise him?" Sam asked.

"We've never seen him before," said Willis.

"That's doubly impossible!" shouted Pike, "There are twenty-three thousand, four hundred and six people in Thistown, they're all on the town register and everybody knows everybody else! When Jonny Ridgewood fell over and knocked himself out on the ridge, three people had reported him missing before he even woke up! We know everyone in Thistown and where they live!""

"We obviously don't." purred Fortuna, "We don't know this No-Life man for a start, do we?

"Well, where did he come from, then?" Pike wanted to know.

"Perhaps he dropped out of the sky." suggested Alice with a grin.

Sam wasn't amused. He prodded the table with his finger. "If there's no life in the No-Life Man, then where has it gone?"

It was a good question and no-one knew the answer. They all looked at each other and shook their heads, except Alice.

"Well," she said, "we know that things disappear in the Cornfields, don't we? Can his life have gone to the Cornfields, do you think?"

No-one answered. It was possible.

"Things do disappear in the Cornfields." said Sam, thinking about it. "But how did his life get out of his body?"

"Did anybody see his life leave him?" asked Alice.

All eyes in the room turned to Belle Fellows who was sitting quietly in a corner behind the witness bench. She shrank back. She didn't like being questioned like this.

"Belle?" said Alice.

She stood up slowly. "No," she said, "I didn't see anything. It was very dark in Duster Alley. That's why I fell over. He was just there on the ground, sort of full of no-life." She sat down again.

"Did any of you see his life go?" Alice the nurse, the doctors and the detective on the witness bench.

"Go where?" asked Willis.

"I don't know," said Alice.

"What you mean like floating through the air?" said Nurse Pine.

"Maybe."

They shook their heads. They hadn't seen anything floating through the air, or anything leaving the No-Life Man's body in any way at all.

"I wonder what it looked like." said Alice.

"You mean,what did his life look like?" asked Fortuna with her head cocked to one side.

"Yes." said Alice. "What colour was it? What shape was it?"

"What shape is his body?" Fortuna asked the doctors. "Is it the same shape as ours?"

Doctor Stitch pushed forward from the crowded bench, "Yes. From the body point of view the No-Life Man is perfectly normal."

"He's a dark olive," said Nurse Pine. "I mean, that's the colour of his skin."

"So was his life dark olive too, do you think?" asked Alice.

"All we know is, it's gone, his life has gone. Somewhere." said Nurse Pine firmly. This was all getting too airy fairy for her.

"And what do you think will happen to him, now that his life has gone?" Sam suddenly asked.

"I imagine he will get stiff from no movement," thought Slice.

"And possibly could start to rot after a while," added Stitch. "No heartbeat you see, to pump round the blood and renew the body. And no breath either....." He stopped and shrugged. "I don't know. We've never seen No-Life before."

"I think we should all go and have a look at him," said Sam being businesslike. "Then at least we'll all know what a No-Life Man looks like."

"Is that an official proposal?" Pike wanted to know. "If it is, we must vote on it. Everybody who thinks we should go, raise their hands...."

But nobody had the time to vote, or even to think about it. Because at that moment there was a loud crash, the great wooden doors of the Town Hall burst open and Ronald Rasper stomped angrily in on his iron leg. He was furious and his black beard shook as he glared at the shocked Assembly Members sitting round their table. Behind him through the broken doors was a great crowd spread out over the Green.

Rasper pointed at the Assembly and roared, "We want the truth!"

AWKWARD CORNER

Ron Rasper was the angriest man in Thistown. He spent most of his time arguing and shouting in the cafes of Awkward Corner (where Avenue A meets the First Circle). Earlier that day, a tall thin and spotty police constable called Chester Brown had been on duty. He'd been crossing the Green when he'd heard angry shouts coming from the red-painted People's Cafe, the third one on the left along from Awkward Corner.

He saw Rasper heaving himself up onto a table outside the Cafe and shouting down at the crowd that was gathering round his feet. It soon became clear to Chester that they'd all heard about the strange Sleeping Man too. Probably from Nurse Pine who never could keep her mouth shut.

Rasper yelled with his loud voice, "We all know about them in the Town Hall. We all know that they don't never tell us nothing!"

Some of the crowd shouted back. "That's right, Rasper."

"And why do they tell us nothing?" Rasper yelled, "because if they keep us in the dark and we don't know nothing, then they can boss us around, can't they?"

"Yes! Rasper's right!" This was Henry Horne who always wore a blue hooped shirt. He was an old friend of Rasper's and with his big funnel shaped mouth and brown teeth, he was just as fierce. "They can boss us around like they always do!"

Rasper went on, "Like this Weird Thing in Duster Alley!" Have they told us anything about him? No they haven't!"

"No they haven't!" Henry Horne repeated everything that Rasper said.

Constable Brown watched from the edge of the crowd which was getting bigger by the second. He wondered if he shouldn't do something.

"Well I've heard no-one recognises him and he doesn't come from Thistown!" Rasper shouted. There were several gasps. "So why haven't they told us anything about him?"

"Why haven't they told us about him?" echoed Henry Horne.

"Because...." Rasper looked down at the angry faces at his feet. "Because they know somethin' about him that we don't!"

"That's right! That's right!"

"But," said Rasper, his voice falling to a whisper, "But this time we're going to find out! This time we are not going to be kept in the dark. Where did this Weird Stranger come from? What's he doing here?" And suddenly he roared, *"And why did he come!""*

"Oh yes! Where, what and why?" yelled Horne.

"Well he obviously came to do *something.* " Rasper went quiet again and looked around the crowd. "What?'

There was a silence. The crowd were sure that Rasper was going to tell them what the Weird Stranger had come for.

"But they won't tell *us* will they? Up there at the Town Hall, they'll only cover up the truth like they always do!"

"Like they always do!" repeated Horne.

"We want the truth!" Rasper yelled.

"The truth! The truth!" The crowd yelled back.

"You should disperse!" Chester Brown had plucked up his courage and climbed onto a chair. He spoke as loudly as he could with his thin, reedy voice, "This is a breach of civic order. Unless this meeting is disbanded, there will be arrests!"

"The truth! The truth!" The crowd ignored him. They knew one policeman couldn't arrest all of them.

"The Town Hall!" roared Rasper.

"The Town Hall!" yelled Horne.

"Let's go to the Town Hall!"

Before Chester could do anything Rasper and Henry Horne had marched off across the Green towards the Town Hall. Chester leapt down from the chair and ran as fast as he could to the police station on Avenue T and the First Circle.

WE WANT THE TRUTH!!

Pike's mouth hung open as Rasper stood in the doorway to the Town Hall. It seemed as if there were hundreds of people behind him all trying to crowd into the assembly chamber. Pike hadn't seen the Green so packed since the last firework display. Then Rasper strode further into the chamber with Henry Horne and the rest of the crowd pushing in behind him.

Pike rose from his seat, "We will not have a meeting of the Town Assembly interrupted! Close the doors!"

Alice and Sam were as shocked as Pike. They'd never seen so many angry people.

"What's made them so angry?" whispered Sam.

"It must be this No-Life Man," said Alice behind her hand.

"Why are they so frightened of him?" Sam couldn't understand it.

"Because they've never seen anything like it before," said Alice, "and people are always scared of things they haven't seen before." She might have added that she was just as scared of what she hadn't seen before as everybody else, but before she could, Rasper roared. "Tell us the truth! We want the *truth!*"

"*The truth!*" yelled the crowd.

"This is a crisis," said Sam sombrely. He nodded his head as if in agreement with himself. "It's a constitutional crisis."

"This," said Fortuna coolly, "is a mob." She'd spoken it loud and didn't seem to care who heard her. Alice had to admire her courage.

Rasper stomped to the end of the Assembly table and stared at the Members one by one. Alice looked straight back at him trying to look as though she found the whole thing very amusing, although the truth was, her knees were knocking together under the table. She knew they had to do something. They couldn't have a crowd like this in the Town Hall. It would be anarchy. Everything would fall apart. She saw that Sam had clasped his hands and was looking down at the table. He was trying to think too. She had an idea. As soon as Rasper looked away from her she reached for a pencil and a piece of paper. She wrote something down quickly.

Pike was till stuttering, "Ww-w-wwill you please c-c-close the door?"

"No." Rasper glared. "We won't close the door, because we've had enough of you keeping us in the dark."

"We're not keeping you in the dark," Sam looked up and said quietly. "There's a public gallery. If you want to go up there, you can see everything we do, and hear everything we say."

"We couldn't all get in there, could we?" Henry Horne said, thinking he was being very funny.

"Well, the newspapers will report everything anyway," said Sam.

" We don't believe newspapers!" Rasper turned and gave Pen and Thrust, the two editors up in the gallery, a dirty look. "We want the truth about this Stranger Man, and we want it *now!*"

"I...." Pike didn't know what to say. He looked up to Rasper and then to the crowd in the doorway, and then back down at the table, which is when he saw the note that Alice had scribbled for him. He glanced up at her and she winked nervously. He read the note again quickly and turned back to Rasper.

"Er.... On behalf of the Assembly, I will address the town from the Town Hall Balcony at seven o'clock tonight. And the truth, as far as we know it, will be told then."

There was a silence, then Rasper said loudly, "That's not good enough! We want to know *now!*"

"We want to know *now!*" yelled Henry Horne in his great foghorn voice and many of the crowd took up the chant, "We want to know *now!*"

"We don't know *now!*"" said Pike getting desperate.

"So why don't we get an Town Assembly who *do know!*" shouted Rasper at the top of his voice to the crowd behind him.

There was a huge roar of approval and it looked as though the crowd were going to invade the Town Hall and Rasper was going to appoint himself Head of the Assembly right there and then.

But he reckoned without Sam, who stood up from the table. His was very tall and he made his voice as strong as he could.

He said, "Wait a minute. And calm down. All of you, calm down. Please." Slowly they stopped shouting and started listening. "The Town Assembly report to the Head of the Assembly, Mr Pike. If you don't like what he says at seven o'clock you can elect a new Town Assembly. That's fair enough isn't it?" He stopped and the crowd thought about it. "After the Mr Pike has spoken, you can listen to Rasper. Then you can agree with who you like."

"That's fair enough!" shouted someone in the crowd. Then someone else repeated it and very soon most of the crowd seemed to think it was a good idea to wait and listen to what Pike had to say later.

Rasper could see he was beaten for now. "Till seven o'clock then!" He spat out the words and stomped out through the crowd, leaving Henry Horne facing the Town Assembly.

"Seven o'clock!" Horne shouted, trying to be as fierce as Rasper.

Then he left and the rest of the crowd quietly followed.

"Well, I have never.....I have never seen...." Pike was too flustered to finish what he was saying.

Fortuna watched as the great doors were closed and at last the mob were outside. "At least we've got a few hours," she said.

"A few hours for what?" whined Pike, "And what am I supposed to say at seven o'clock?"

"That's not the problem, is it?" said Fortuna, her black eyes getting very hard. "Once they find out that this stranger is a No-Life Man. They'll all want to know where he came from, and why he's here, and where his life went to, won't they? Like we do. How are we supposed to tell you what to say if we don't know ourselves?"

"Let's go and look at him," said Sam slowly.

"Yes," said Fortuna and most of the rest of the Assembly nodded. "So that's what we'll do. At the Hospital, three o'clock," she said. "And don't be late."

Fortuna spoke as though she was the Head of the Assembly. Alice looked at Sam again. Her smile was gone now. It was the first time that Sam had ever seen Alice Bright looking entirely serious.

"We'll do exactly what Fortuna has suggested," said Pike, relieved that someone had told him what to do. "Assembly dissolved," and he slumped back in his chair with his long nose almost touching his chin he was so out of his depth.

They all slowly left the chamber. Alice went out with Sam, and Fortuna left on her own. They were all shocked. They'd never seen a mob on the Green before. They'd never seen a mob *anywhere* before.

"Everybody is being so angry!" said Alice as she stood with Sam at the bottom of the steps.

"Yes," he said, "It's all different now."

"What do you mean?"

"Here. In Thistown. It feels different."

"And all because of some stupid No-Life Man!"

"He must have come from somewhere," said Sam.

"Where?"

Sam shrugged.

"I'm going to look around." said Alice.

"What for?"

"I don't know, do? Find another No-Life Man! Or Woman!"

She stormed off across the Green leaving Sam standing outside the Town Hall, staring up at the bluebirds in the Oak trees. They were pecking and shrieking louder than ever.

THE POLICE STATION

At around the same time, Chester Brown sat in the Police canteen. He looked down at the silver buttons of his uniform and half-heartedly shone one of them up a bit with the cuff of his jacket. He was depressed and his thin, wiry body was hunched over his plate of indigestible police food. As he shovelled it in he thought of how he'd described the events at Awkward Corner to the Chief of Police and tried to convince him that there'd been a crisis at the Town Hall.

The Chief a big and lazy man (Fat slob if you asked Chester) had laughed loudly. "Crisis? What crisis? And anyway what would we do if there was one?"

Then he'd patted Chester on the back and gone up to his office for a lie down on his sofa under the window.

Chester knew that at least in part, the Chief was right. There wasn't much he could do, even if there was a crisis. Thistown didn't have a very large police force because there were hardly any crimes to solve. The main duty of the Chief of Police was to look good in his uniform and walk behind the Head of the Assembly as he opened the doors of the Town Hall every morning. This made Chester even more worried. He had this feeling that something was about to happen and there was going to be very little he or the Thistown Police could do about it.

EATING WITH SAM

Sam's house was a mess but he never noticed it. He was always too busy thinking about other things. Mainly how to make something or invent something or at least work on something. He liked to think of himself as a bit of a designer. So his house, including his kitchen was always full of half finished objects made out of paper or cardboard or wood. He stood in the middle of of it all and put another three big potatoes to the pan and decided to fry an extra egg. He wondered why he was cooking so much. He knew that when Alice would come back to house from wherever she'd been because she always did on Assembly days, and then she'd only eat a bit of lettuce and if she was hungry, a tomato, so he was cooking mainly for himself. So why was he boiling so many spuds? I'm starving, he thought as he added another one. Maybe it's the air today, or maybe it's the shock of what happened at the Town Hall?

He took a bite out of an apple as he stirred the potatoes with a wooden spoon. His hunger annoyed him because he was trying to remember something and it was getting in the way (Alice hadn't been joking when she'd talked about Sam remembering everything. Everybody knew that he had the most incredible memory, the longest memory, a memory as big as his head. He could remember when the houses of Thistown were made of wood before they were brick; he could remember when they trained the first donkey and chained him to a cart; he could even remember when Old Pen had been elected as Head of the Town Assembly, which was exactly seven hundred and fifty three years ago.) Now he concentrated as hard as he could. He was trying to remember if there'd ever been anything like a No-Life Man in Thistown before.

"No, can't remember anything like it at all," he said to himself.

There was a bang at the door. He turned, expecting Alice, and instead Belle Fellows came tumbling in. She only just avoided falling over Sam's half built new invention of a wooden collapsible bed which was standing by the door.

"I'm starving," she said.

"I haven't got enough," said Sam standing in front of the stove

"Yes you have," said Belle, peering round him and seeing the spuds in the pan. "You've got about nine!"

"Well, Alice is...."

"She never eats anything." said Belle sitting down. "She's too skinny."

Reluctantly Sam wiped two plates with an old rag and put them on the table.

"Oh very clean," said Belle as she tucked into Sam's dinner. She held up the hand that Nurse Pine had bandaged in the Hospital, "My cut won't go. I've fallen over hundreds of times and had thousands of cuts and grazes and they usually heal up in no time, but this one won't."

"Yes, well, there are a lot of things that are very strange.... Sam stopped. Halfway through the sentence his voice had gone up to a high-pitched squeak and then fallen to a kind of deep gravely bark.

"Why are you talking like that?" asked Belle.

"I don't know." said Sam as his voice shot right up again.

Belle laughed. "Your voice is the funniest thing that's happened all day!"

Sam, confused though he was, had to laugh too. And just for a second, they felt like it was the old Thistown where everybody laughed at everything. And then they stopped laughing and looked at each other across the table, because they knew it wasn't. Sam's voice was playing tricks and Belle's cut wouldn't heal. Why? They were looking at each other in a puzzled way when Alice came in.

She looked at the two of them sitting at the table and said simply, "I know. There's something wrong isn't there?"

"Is there?" asked Sam, still not sure about it.

"There definitely is," Alice said. "I've just been up to Awkward Corner. I'm starving, can I have something to eat?"

"You're hungry too?" said Belle with her eyes wide. "Something must be very, very wrong."

"What was at Awkward Corner?" asked Sam as he found another plate and a dirty fork.

"You're not going to like it."

"The potatoes and eggs?" asked Belle.

"No, what I'm going to tell you."

"What happened?" said Sam.

"Well, I went into the People's cafe and asked Leo for a juice as usual, but then I wanted some food too, so I asked him for a sandwich and he said he didn't have anything because they'd sold out because everyone was hungry today."

"Everyone?" asked Belle. "Everyone is hungry?" She turned to Sam. "See. That's what we were saying. Everybody in the whole town is starving!"

"Is this what you've come to tell us?" asked Sam. He was a bit grumpy because Alice and Belle were eating too much of his food.

"Wait a minute and I'll tell you," said Alice. "I was just about to go when I heard a voice coming through the door of a room at the back of the cafe. It was Rasper. You can't make a mistake with his voice can you? He was arguing with someone. I heard him say," she mimicked his gruff voice, "I know all that, but it's time a few changes were made around here, and we're going to make them.'" She acted it out, prodding the air with her finger like she imagined Rasper would have done.

"What changes?" asked Belle.

"Who's going to make them?" said Sam.

"Well him and... then I heard this voice like a foghorn. It was Henry Horne. You can't mistake him either, can you? He said, that's right, and we're going to make them. So them two. But then Rasper said, and you have to make up your mind, whether you're with us or against us!"

"Who had to make up their mind?" Sam had stopped eating. He held his fork in mid air.

"It's obvious, Sam," said Belle.

"Who?"

"Someone else was in the back room with them!"

"I know that, Belle. Who was it?"

"I don't know," said Alice before Belle could say anything else, "because at that moment the door closed and I didn't hear anymore. So I asked Leo who it was. He just put his finger to his lips and gave me this." She reached into her shoulder bag and pulled out a newspaper. "This is the bit you won't like."

"I didn't like the first bit much," said Sam.

He could see the long black, blaring bugle on the top of the paper and realised immediately it was a copy of The Clarion. Alice spread it out on the table between them. And Sam definitely didn't like it. In fact it was the most terrible thing he'd ever read. Written in huge, black letters was the headline, ***ENEMIES OF THISTOWN!*** And underneath was a photograph of every member of the Town Assembly. There was Sam with his round glasses making his eyes seem huge; Alice with her mouth open looking stupid; Fortuna in a sulky pose and more like a cat than ever; Pike, who you could hardly see because his nose was so big, and even old Croker who had his hand cupped round his ear. They all looked ridiculous.

"The enemies of Thistown?" Sam looked up Alice, "What are they talking about? I'm not an enemy. How could I be? I live in here!"

Alice read out from the paper, "These people have become our enemies because they are hiding the truth of the Strange No-Life Man."

"We don't know the truth ourselves." said Sam sounding upset. To be called an enemy at all was bad enough, but to have it announced on the front page of a newspaper with a silly picture of yourself, was just too much. He got up and walked angrily round the kitchen.

Alice carried on reading from the paper. "We have a right to know! Are the members of the Town Assembly using this No-Life Man for their own purposes?"

"Our own purposes? What purposes?" Sam couldn't believe it.

"Listen to this," Alice went on, "Are they using the No-Life Man to take over Thistown? We know that there are strong connections between several members of the Town Assembly and Editor Pen of the Opinion Newspaper, who is always writing favourably about them."

"Why should they have a go at Old Pen as well?" asked Sam. "What's he got to do with it?"

"Because they know that he never agrees with the Clarion," said Alice. "And so they're getting at him, before he gets at them." She folded the newspaper. "As soon as I read it in the cafe, I was really furious, and so I decided to find out what was going on. I wanted to know who Rasper and Henry Horne had been talking to in the back room, so I went to the door and banged on it."

"Who answered?" Belle's eyes were round.

"No-one."

"So what did you do?"

"I opened it."

"You opened the door?"

"Yes."

"Who was there?"

"No-one. The room was empty."

"So we'll never find out who they were talking to," said Belle.

"And who it was Rasper said had to be with them or against them." added Sam. "Unless it was editor Thrust of the Clarion." He banged his hand on the table. He wanted to screw up the paper. He was more upset than he could remember. And with his memory that meant a very long time.

"No, it wasn't editor Thrust," said Alice. "He was already on their side because the paper was already printed."

"Well who, then?" asked Sam.

"I don't know," said Alice, "but I'm sure we'll find out. Fortuna was outside the cafe when I came out. If you think you're angry you should have seen her when she saw the paper. She thought everyone was corngone."

"There is one thing we can do," said Sam, finally beginning to think properly. "If they're that worried about the Opinion, why don't we go and ask Editor Pen if he'll print that we're not Enemies of Thistown!" He prodded the copy of the Clarion again. "I mean everybody will read this and think it's true!"

"I'll go and see him," said Alice with a smile. This had all got her down, but the prospect of seeing her old friend, Editor Pen cheered her up. "Don't worry, I know he'll be on our side!" she said as she jumped up from her chair up and stepped straight into a cardboard model of Sam's design for a new Town Hall. She looked down on it, squashed on the floor. "Oh sorry, Sam."

THE CORNFIELDS

The Assembly were to see the No-Life Man at three o'clock which meant Sam had an hour to fill before he went up to the Hospital for the inspection. He decided to go and have a sit under the oak trees on the Green, but after he'd come out of his house and walked the few yards on the Fifth Circle to Avenue R, he found himself turning right towards the cornfields instead of left towards the Green. He wanted to think about things, and like everyone else in Thistown, when it was time to ponder, he went to the corn and stared at the vast yellow fields.

He sat on the Edge at the top of Avenue R with his arms wrapped round his knees and looked out at it waving in the distance as far as the horizon. Where did it end? Where did it begin? Why couldn't they cross it? Fortuna had said that she thought the people on Awkward Corner were 'corngone.' He knew what she meant. They were gone to corn, or in other words, mad. And perhaps they were like that because they couldn't bear to be trapped anymore by these silent, everlasting fields that surrounded them. Sam knew how they felt and half got up before the corn drove him corngone too, but then he sat down again. He'd remembered something.

There was a time around a hundred years before when a small group of men had become so desperate to see if there was anything beyond the corn that they decided to build a tower on the Edge by Avenue A to look out over it. They took years and years and built it as high as they possibly could. When it was completed they looked out from the top for days, but could see nothing other than more and more corn from horizon to horizon. After a while, two of the men went corngone and one sunny day they ran down the steps of the Tower, straight into the corn and disappeared.

And then twenty years ago there was the worst time of all when a Head of the Town Assembly called Reggie Run had gone corngone. Sam remembered, Run had been a bit odd for weeks and then all of a sudden decided to speak to the whole town from the Town Hall balcony. He said that he'd been watching the corn for days and he'd seen that there were certain times when the wind blew a path across it. The wind didn't last long, he said, but if anyone who really wanted to was ready to go at any minute, and they were fast enough, they could travel along that path and they'd get through the cornfields to the other side before the wind blew again and the path closed.

There was a great debate. Sam had been part of it and like most people had dismissed the idea. But there were many who didn't and Reggie Run had set up a great camp for them on the Green. They'd called themselves the Corn Travellers. They all had their bags packed and were ready to go at a moments notice. Look-outs were sent to the end of every Avenue to see when and where the wind would blow the path. At the end of Avenue A was the favourite because it was the widest. They waited for the wind.

It was a very unhappy time. There were many arguments among friends as to whether they should go or not. Sam had stood on the Green arguing that it was a stupid idea because no-one knew how far they'd have to go before they'd crossed the cornfields, and no-one knew either how long the wind would blow. But there were many who were just too desperate to see what what was on the other side. Sometimes Sam knew just how they felt. He remembered sadly that there were many tearful farewells every night and every morning because everyone knew that the Corn Travellers would have no time to say goodbye once the wind blew.

Then one day it had grown dark. No-one spoke. It was as if they knew it was the time. The wind was just a breeze at first, cool and refreshing on their faces, but then it blew harder, and then harder, and finally a lookout on the roof of the Town Hall shouted, "The path! The path! It's at the end of Avenue M!"

Run moved quickly up the Avenue that would be known from that day on as 'Corn Travellers Way.' The rest followed. Some with small bags, others with huge suitcases, even one pulling a donkey and a high loaded, heavy cart.

When Run reached the top of the Avenue, he looked out, and sure enough in the light of the low sun there was a path cut across the corn by the wind. He turned back to his followers. "Now!" he shouted. "Goodbye Thistown! We love you all! When the next wind comes, join us!"

With that, he ran into the cornfields. It seemed as if he was right. The corn seemed to part before him and he didn't disappear. With a huge roar, the others followed; walking, running, heaving their cases and carts. Soon there was a long line of people stretched out as far as the eye could see across the Cornfields and another line of their friends along the Edge hoping against hope that the path would remain open.

Sam sat with tears in his eyes as he remembered a woman called Maggie Blush with her blond hair piled high on her head, who had decided to go at the last minute and tagged onto the end of the line. She was the last anyone saw of any of them.

With a howl the wind suddenly changed. There were cries all along the Edge as they yelled for the Corn Travellers to get back. Some of them felt the wind twist themselves and started to fling themselves back towards Thistown. But it was too late, they couldn't run faster than the wind and the Cornfields swallowed them.

Maggie Blush hadn't gone far when she turned back and so she was close to the Edge when the corn caught up with her. Sam could see her, even now, as she dived back towards the safety of the Edge, her eyes bulging in terror and her mouth contorted in an awful scream, but it was too late, the remorseless corn covered her, all except one hand that she'd flung out across the Edge trying to reach back. It lay there on the Edge cut off at the wrist, with a silver ring sparkling on the second finger. Sam had watched with a pale and shocked face as someone took a stick and pushed it back into the yellow. It disappeared immediately. No-one moved. The wind had dropped and the corn swayed beautifully again in the soft sunlight.

There was no sound at all apart from a muffled sobbing all along the Edge.

Sam dabbed his eyes with his handkerchief as he thought of it. He'd lost many friends that day. He looked up at the corn rippling peacefully in front of him and wondered how Thistown started in the middle of it all? He didn't know. Even his incredible memory couldn't remember that far back. In the beginning, it seemed, there was no beginning. He got up slowly and turned back towards the Green. Whatever editor Thrust and The Clarion had to say about it, he was a member of the Town Assembly and it was time to inspect the No-Life Man in the Hospital.

A SECOND OPINION

Alice had gone to the Opinion Offices and seen Old Pen. He'd been more than happy to run a special issue of the Opinion, in fact he'd been so offended by the Clarion's accusations of bias against him that he'd decided to write a stinging editorial in reply before Alice had come.

"On second thoughts," said Alice as she looked round the old print room with its peeling paint and ancient presses, "Perhaps we should wait until after we've seen the No-Life Man? That could change everything. And who wants a paper that's out of date. It's only good for lighting fires, isn't it?"

Pen agreed that it was better to hang on. "Alright," he said, "I'll hold the presses." Then he groaned.

"What's the matter?" asked Alice.

"It's my back," said Pen, grimacing and trying to stretch. "I've got back ache. I've never had that before. Why should I suddenly have it now?"

"I don't know," said Alice, thinking about it. "It's strange isn't it? Belle's cut won't heal, Sam's voice is going funny, we're all hungry all the time, and now your back aches. What's happening to us, do you think?"

"The last time I had back ache," said Pen, "was fifty years ago, when I tried to move that press on my own." He eyed a particularily heavy looking piece of machinery in the centre of the print room. "But I certainly haven't tried to shift anything recently. To tell you the truth, I've been feeling too tired."

"I've never noticed you looking tired before," said Alice respectfully, deciding not to mention the huge bags under her old friend's eyes.

"Anyway," said Pen, not wishing to prolong this kind of talk, "we should get down to the Hospital."

NO-LIFE STINKS

"There they are." Alice pointed ahead to where Sam, Fortuna and the rest of the Assembly had gathered on the grass outside the red doors of the Hospital on the First Circle and Avenue Q.

"We're waiting for the doctors," said Sam as she came up with Pen.

"And they're late," said Fortuna impatiently, at which moment the clock on the Town Hall struck three, the Hospital's doors opened and Stitch and Slice came out.

"Looks like they're on time," said Alice with a grin as Fortuna pursed her lips.

"This way," said Stitch or Slice and motioned for all ten members of the Assembly to follow them inside.

"This is all a waste of time," moaned Pike. His nose had begun to drip and he wiped it on the back of his sleeve. "A complete waste of...."

But no-one bothered to answer him. They trooped in through the doors. He hurried after them, still moaning, and found them all facing a pair of of double doors at the back of the hospital.

"This is where he is," said one of the doctors as the other one opened the doors. He went into the room beyond and turned on a low blue light.

Everyone filed into the room, not knowing quite what to expect. What did a No-Life Man look like? Sam felt strangely nervous and was having to admit to himself that he didn't like things to change too much. Alice on the other hand was excited and eager to find out what was new. She was the first into the room and the first to the table that stood in the middle of it. She stopped and looked down. There in front of her, lying under a white sheet, was the No-Life man. She could see his contours quite clearly. The doctors waited for the rest of the Assembly to gather round the table and then took hold of a corner of the sheet each and slowly pulled it away.

The No-Life Man lay on his back. His arms were by his side and his eyes were closed. He wore a black and white striped shirt and dark blue trousers. Alice looked at his face. His hair was black and swept back from his forehead. And he was grinning.

Alice looked at Sam. She could tell that the No-Life Man's grin had scared him as much as it had her. It was fixed as though someone had moulded it out of clay, except of course that his face was olive but it had gone white. Very white. They'd never seen a face as white as that. He looked a bit like a clown.

Pike broke the silence. "I told you it was a waste of time," he said, but he was as affected by the sight of the perfectly still, olive white and grinning No-Life Man as everyone else.

Fortuna suddenly hissed, "What's that stink?"

Alice wrinkled her nose. Fortuna was right. There was a horrible smell in the room. It seemed to be getting worse as they all stood there.

"I feel sick," groaned Pike.

"He's beginning to rot," said Stitch.

"Take these," Slice handed out small white hospital towels which they put over their mouths.

Sam tried not to breathe as he looked down on the No-Life Man. He was sure he'd seen him somewhere before. He racked his brains but couldn't work out where.

He said, "Is there anything in his pockets?"

"Not when he came in," said Nurse Pine.

"Why are his feet so clean?" asked Alice. She was looking carefully at a pair of spotless heels.

"I didn't wash them, I can assure you of that," said Nurse Pine defensively. "They were like that when he came in."

"Isn't Duster Alley dirty?" Alice looked round.

"You're saying someone put him there?" asked Fortuna catching on as quickly as she usually did.

"They must have done," said Alice, "or he'd have got his feet dirty, wouldn't he?"

She glanced at Sam. He was thinking about it too.

"Who cares! If I stay in this stink anymore, I'll puke!" And as if to prove his point Pike started retching right there and then. He stumbled to the door with his towel held tight to his mouth.

"So will I! And me!" Several other members of the Assembly went out after him, and finally Alice and Fortuna had to follow.

Alice turned back. Sam was still staring down at the No-Life Man's face.

"Come on, Sam. It's horrible in here!"

"I'm sure I've seen him somewhere." Sam walked quickly out of the room and they joined the others who were gulping down the clean air coming in through an open window at the front of the building.

"Well that didn't help at all, did it?" Pike glared at everyone. "Now we've seen him, what great announcement am I going to make at seven o'clock?"

No-one knew how to answer. Most of them were feeling too sick to even try.

"The point isn't the No-Life Man!" said Fortuna angrily. She walked away from the window and stood on her own at the side of the room. "It's Rasper." she hissed. "It's Rasper who's the big problem, isn't it?" She had a look on her face as if she was going to make Rasper pay for it personally. It was a look Alice would remember later.

"And what do I tell them all tonight?" wailed Pike.

Alice suddenly said, "Oh that's easy."

Fortuna turned and snapped, "You think so? So why don't you tell us?"

Alice said, "I will if you give me a chance, Fortuna." She turned to Pike. "I think you should get up on the Town Hall balcony and simply tell everyone that we are going to put the No-Life man back where he belongs."

Pike said, "Oh yes? And in your high and exalted opinion, where exactly does the No-Life Man belong?"

"It's obvious." Alice shrugged her shoulders. "In the Cornfields. He hasn't got any life, and he stinks, and so he's no use to any of us, so we may as well put him in the corn where he'll disappear. And so will the problem."

"Ahem. I really don't know..." Pike looked around to see if anyone else agreed with Alice.

Fortuna suddenly smiled and said silkily, "I think that's a very good idea. Well done, Alice. We do that and Rasper will have to shut up, won't he?"

"Oh I still don't know," Pike whined.

But everyone else agreed and several of them patted Alice on the back. Now they wouldn't have to answer any of those awkward questions. The problem, as she said, would just disappear. They all filed out. Only Sam remained. He wasn't sure whether he wanted to put the No-Life Man in the corn or not. It would certainly get rid of him, but then they'd never find out who he was, would they? And he didn't like things to be left unresolved. The corn was a big enough mystery in their lives. He didn't want another one.

GETTING THE PAPER OUT

As Alice walked across the Green towards the Opinion building to bring out the next edition of the paper she saw Fortuna telling Pike exactly what he had to say on the balcony that night. She was being as forceful as usual but Pike didn't seem to want to listen and Alice couldn't help wondering why he was being so awkward about it. To get rid of the No-Life Man by throwing him in the corn was the obvious answer. So what was Pike's problem? A horrible thought suddenly struck her. Was he the mystery person in the back room of the People's cafe who Rasper had been trying to persuade? No, it couldn't be. Pike was an elected member of the Town Assembly and he wouldn't listen to someone like Rasper. Or would he? She put the thought out of her mind as she joined Pen in the Opinion office.

"Mr Pen," she said, "can we just write down everything that's happened fairly and honestly so that everyone can read it and make up their own mind?"

"That's all a good newspaper ever does." said Pen. "People can only solve problems if they have the correct information."

"Good," said Alice thinking about it. So what about, *Let's Face the Facts,* as a headline?"

Pen laughed, "Why not indeed, Alice?"

They began to work together on the front page article. Alice wrote most of it. She clearly and honestly told what had happened in the Town Hall that day and then what they'd seen at the hospital. She decided not to say that they would be throwing the No-Life Man in the corn as that would spoil the surprise of what Pike would announce later from the Town Hall balcony.

As she did this Pen concentrated on all the other stories of the day. There'd been a woman who'd tried to pick flowers at the disused goldmine and fallen down the lift shaft. She'd had to be rescued by the Thistown fire service. And then there was the award to be given to Lennie Leather for exactly two hundred years service in the donkey stables; and then there were the sports pages at the back, and then there were.... It was quite enough for an man who was eighty-five, had always been eighty-five.... and he had backache too.

They worked for the rest of the afternoon. Alice helped Pen set up the presses in the print room, and watched them roll as hundreds of copies of The Opinion were printed and stacked at the end of the room. She helped parcel them up and hand them out to the vendors who'd been rounded up for the special edition. As the last one left with a bulging newspaper bag, she was about to sit down for a rest when she heard footsteps on the stairs. It was Sam coming up from the Green below.

"Bit late, aren't you?" said Alice. "Mr Pen and me, we've...." She looked over at the old editor who was fast asleep in his chair. "We've done it all now."

"Oh,' said Sam, not realising that he was supposed to have read Alice's mind and come up three hours ago to give her a hand. "We didn't come for that anyway."

"We? Who's we?"

"Hullo Alice," Miriam Marjorami appeared in the doorway. She was a friend of Sam's. "Mister Pike will be giving his announcement soon, won't he?" Miriam was the same age as them, had huge grey eyes, a mass of soft, curly black hair and golden brown skin. She spoke in a low voice and liked to move slowly and carefully. She thought that touching things or smelling them was just as important as seeing or hearing. Her house was full of scents and perfumes and what she liked to imagine were mysterious potions for healing. She wore a long coloured skirt which she tucked under her legs as she sat in a chair by the window. "It's the best view from here." She said softly as she looked down at the Green below. It seemed as if half of Thistown was gathering under the oak trees. "Look, there are hundreds of them." Her huge eyes widened in amazement.

"It's more like thousands," said Alice. "Mr Pen, wake up!"

"And they've all come to hear Mr Pike?" Miriam could hardly believe that anyone would be so interested.

"Yes, and he's such an old idiot," said Alice.

Pen managed to shake himself awake and Sam moved the old man's chair over to the window so he could see better. He looked down at the crowd where the newspaper vendors were moving quickly through the crowd and said, "Alice, they're all reading the Opinion!"

Alice looked down and felt quite proud of herself. She wondered about helping out with the paper more often. She looked down at the Green. It was very satisfying to see hundreds of people reading what she had written, all at the same time. But even better was the fact that the mood seemed to be changing down there. It had started off quite sombrely as the people had gathered, not really knowing what was going on, but now they had the facts from the Opinion they were beginning to relax. Some were laughing and it was getting more lively by the minute. Even the Town Band had struck up and before long a boring old Town Meeting was starting to feel more like a carnival.

"It's going to be alright, Alice!" said Old Pen, smiling, "We're going to be able to put this dreadful No-Life Man right behind us."

"Especially when Pike tells them what we're going to do with him," said Sam.

"My idea," said Alice.

"I know, Alice," said Sam wearily. He'd decided that all things considered, she was right, and it would be better to dump the No-Life Man once and for all.

"There's Chester," said Sam.

Chester Brown, Detective Willis and several other policemen, including even the Chief of Police, were standing around the edge of the crowd, looking untroubled and happy.

"It's one minute to seven." Alice said, looking up at the Town Hall clock.

"I'm looking forward to this." said Miriam. "And after can we have some peace again please?"

The Opinion offices were next but two to the the Town Hall and the window they watched through was the same height as the balcony. They could see clearly as the Town Browncoat Boys fixed up a microphone by the balcony rail. The crowd below began to settle.

"Mr Pike will be on his way," said Miriam.

"I only hope he listened to Fortuna." For a reason she couldn't quite understand, Alice was beginning to get worried.

Just as the clock struck seven, Sam pointed down to the crowd closest to the Town Hall. "Look. It's Rasper!"

RASPER'S NOSE

Ronald Rasper, Henry Horne and a large group from Awkward Corner were pushing their way through toward the huge doors of the Town Hall. Even from where they were they could hear the sound of Rasper's iron leg as it stomped up the steps. He shoved the doors open with his burly shoulder and his gang followed him inside.

"What are they doing?" Alice looked at the rest of them.

"He's going to speak after Pike, remember?" said Sam.

"But that doesn't mean he has to barge into the Town Hall, does it?"

The clock showed a minute past seven. They waited. Then two minutes past. They waited. And then five past. And nothing happened.

"I don't like this," said Alice.

"I don't like it either," said Sam.

They could see that the crowd down below were getting restless.

And then it was ten past seven, and still no Pike.

"It must be Rasper," said Alice.

"You mean he's stopping Pike coming out?" asked Sam. "He can't do that. Pike is head of the Assembly."

Alice thought again of the possibility that it might have been Pike who she'd heard Rasper talking to in the back room of the People's cafe, but decided not to say anything yet.

"What *is* going on?" asked Miriam.

The townspeople below were now getting anxious. All day they'd been hearing and reading different things about the No-Life Man and the Town Assembly. Now they wanted the Head of the Town Assembly to tell them exactly what had been happening. Some of them began to jeer and whistle, and then there was the beginning of a slow handclap.

"I'm going to go and see what's going on," said Alice, but as she rose from her chair, there was a cheer from certain sections of the crowd. Rasper had appeared on the Town Hall balcony.

"Rasper?" Sam couldn't believe it. 'He's supposed to speak *after* Pike. Not *before*. That was the agreement."

Rasper went up to the microphone. "Good people of Thistown, we apologise for the delay."

"*We* apologise?" said Sam. "What's he mean? *We?* Rasper isn't one of the Town Assembly, is he? So how can he be talking about *we?*" He was outraged already.

"However," Rasper went on, "The Head of the Assembly, Percy Pike will now speak."

"Well at least it's Pike who's going to speak first," said Alice.

"Second," said Sam. "Rasper spoke first."

Alice looked at him. She could see he was very worried about what was happening.

There was a great cheer as Pike came to the microphone. He grinned horribly and was about to speak, but before he could open his mouth Rasper grabbed the microphone back again and shouted, "At eleven o'clock this morning, the old Assembly threw the people out of the Town Hall!"

"What's he talking about? *Old* Assembly?" Sam looked round angrily.

Rasper went on, "As the people always have a right to hear what the Town Assembly say, this was clearly a breach of the rules by certain Members of the Assembly, who took no notice of their Head of Assembly, Pike, who wanted us to stay!"

"That's rubbish!" Alice shouted, "Pike was as relieved as the rest of us when we got rid of Rasper!"

"Today, I met with Pike..." said Rasper.

"So that's it!" said Alice. "So it *was* Pike that Rasper was talking to in the back of the People's cafe!"

"Pike? Are you serious?" Sam couldn't believe it.

"It's obvious, Pike has joined up with them. And that's why he wasn't happy about the plan to throw the No-Life man back into the Cornfields. Because he didn't know what Rasper would think of it!"

As if to prove her right Rasper shouted into the microphone, "I have spoken with Head of the Assembly Pike, and we have agreed that as the old Assembly broke the rules, a new Assembly must be formed. Pike, because he has fully co-operated with us, will remain on the Assembly, but not as Head. I, Rasper, am the head of the new Assembly!"

"He can't do that, it's unconstitutional!" said Sam.

And there was silence in the crowd too as they tried to work out whether this was a good idea or not. Rasper hadn't been elected, but as the Town Assembly never did anything much, then what did it matter?

"And now, good people of Thistown!" said Rasper, "Pike will speak."

Pike stepped nervously forward with his silly nose in the air.

"Look at him. He's no more than Rasper's nose!" said Alice scornfully.

Pike was looking at a piece of paper in his hand. It quickly became obvious that it was a speech that Rasper had written for him.

"First," he said, "I want to congratulate Rasper on becoming Head of the Town Assembly." He looked towards Rasper who smiled his horrible smile and motioned for Pike to carry on. "The rest of the Assembly will be announced tomorrow!"

There were a few cheers. If Pike had said it was alright, then it must be.

Sam was outraged. "An Assembly can't be just announced. It has to be elected!"

Henry Horne started to clap and shout as loud as he could. Of course other people from Awkward Corner joined in. "Rasper! Rasper!" they chanted.

Rasper stepped up to the Microphone again. "The one thing I promise you is that the New Assembly will tell you the truth about the No-Life Man!" he yelled, "I will tell you the whole truth!"

The crowd from Awkward Corner began to clap. "The whole truth!"

More in the crowd were applauding.

"Look!" said Alice pointing down. "Even Nurse Pine is clapping.

"And so is Detective Willis!" said Sam.

"And I will tell you what the No-Life Man has to say to us!" Rasper went on.

There was a silence as the crowd took this in.

Pen laughed. "What fools. How can a No-Life Man have anything to say?"

Rasper carried on, "You see, it is most likely that the No-Life Man is a messenger!"

"A messenger!" repeated Horne.

"A messenger!" The words went quickly round the crowd. "Where from?" shouted someone.

"Why else would he have come if it wasn't to tell us something?" yelled Rasper, ignoring the question.

"We should listen to the messenger!" shouted Horne.

"We should listen to him!" The crowd took up the chant.

Rasper raised his hands. The crowd went quiet. "This Message has come to us in a strange way, and perhaps not everyone will be able to understand it," he said. "But when we on the new Assembly know what it means, we shall tell the People of Thistown the whole and absolute truth! Because one thing is for certain!" He stopped and made everyone wait, "The message of the No-Life Man will bring great changes to Thistown!"

Then the whole crowd applauded. Among others Nurse Pine, Detective Willis and even the Chief of Police shouted their approval. A chant began, "The No-Life Man will change Thistown forever!"

"Oh no he won't!" said Alice grimly as she turned away from the window.

"Alice?" said Sam. "Where are you...."

But Alice had already gone. The only answer Sam received was the slamming of the print room door. Sam sighed. It was typical of Alice to rush away just as she was most needed.

"It's like they're all corngone." Miriam was staring wide-eyed at the madly chanting crowd.

" *The No-Life Man will change everything!*" It seemed as if the whole town was echoing with the roar.

"There's Alice." Miriam pointed down to the Green. Alice was at the edge of the crowd, talking quietly to the doctors Stitch and Slice. They slipped away together under the darkness of the trees.

Someone in the crowd shouted. "Long Live the No-Life Man!"

Pen laughed again, "Did you hear that!"

"Can you believe it?" Sam shouted incredulously, "Long live the No-Life man! They're definitely corngone!"

"And they will get worse." said Old Pen, "You mark my words, much worse."

After a while the noise below them stopped. Rasper had raised his arms one last time and the crowd dispersed. Sam and Miriam left Pen in the printroom and walked across the Green. They could still hear the last of them singing excitedly in the Avenues as they made their way home. "Long live the No-life Man. Long live the No-Life....." And finally it was quiet.

"So much for the Opinion," said Sam sadly as he looked round at the hundreds of copies of the paper with its headline ***Let's Face the Facts***, thrown down all over the grass.

"Rasper's done it now, hasn't he?" said Sam. "We've all been thrown off the Town Assembly and that's that."

"Rasper's a liar and he's lied to them." Fortuna walked out from the darkness of the trees. She'd been in the crowd and seen everything. "And they're so stupid that they believe everything he said."

"It's the No-Life Man," said Miriam. "You see, he's disturbed us because we don't understand him."

"I don't care about him! I don't like being thrown off assemblies, and that's that!" said Fortuna angrily. "No-one does that to me!"

"No-one should do that to any of us," said Sam gloomily.

"It looks like Mr Rasper has got what he wanted, doesn't it?" said Miriam sadly. "And he's so ugly."

RASPER RULES

The next day Ron Rasper stood in front of the new Town Assembly in the Town Hall. He was very pleased with himself and pulled himself up to his full height, which as he was more square than tall, wasn't very much. He grinned his horrible gap-toothed grin and ran his stubby fingers through his knotted beard as he looked around at his new Assembly, or gang, as he privately called them.

Pike was trying to appear important but actually looked small and crumpled as he tried to stop the stream that poured from his nose. He was convinced it was getting worse and had even considered going up to the Hospital for some kind of noseplug treatment. Henry Horne sat proudly next to him, his huge mouth fixed permanently in an arrogant sneer. Bill Rory, another follower of Rasper sat opposite him. Rory was like a big grey rock with a huge chin and overgrown bushy eyebrows. He was grunting and leering as he looked over the shoulder of Editor Thrust of the Clarion.

"You write what yer told to write," said Rory belligerently as he stubbed a filthy finger at Thrust's notebook. "Understand?"

Thrust tried to look disdainful, but editor Pen of the Opinion who was, as usual, up in the gallery, was pleased to see that Thrust was beginning to wish he'd never joined Rasper.

The other Members of the Assembly were either thugs from Awkward Corner, or respected but weak townspeople who thought that at last they would have a moment of glory with Rasper. They all watched he as he clumped up and down around them. They were all remembering the night before, when he'd made the whole town cheer his every word.

Sam and Fortuna sat by Pen in the gallery. The new Assembly disgusted him "They'd sit up and beg with their tongues hanging out if Rasper wanted them to," he said.

"I should be down there," hissed Fortuna with a voice like an angry cat. "Look at that snot-nosed clown, Percy Pike. We should never have let him be Head of the Assembly in the first place!"

"Keep your voice down," said Sam, lowering his.

"Where's Alice?" asked Fortuna looking around.

"Oh she's doing something," Sam always defended Alice although he wasn't sure why.

"Doing what?"

"I don't know." Sam had to admit he hadn't seen Alice since she'd disappeared from the Green with Stitch and Slice the night before.

"Never where she's needed, is she?" said Fortuna angrily.

"No," said Sam. He looked away from her blazing eyes.

"The people of Thistown should see the No-life Man!" Rasper was shouting down below, "After all, let's face it, he's come here for them!"

"How does he know that?" Sam clenched his knuckles. He was so frustrated. Everything Rasper said was nonsense, but somehow everybody seemed to believe him.

The Assembly Members certainly did. They all solemnly nodded their agreement.

"I say we put him up on the old Tower by the Edge on Avenue B!" Rasper said and no-one dared disagree. "Don't forget the Tower was built to look out over the cornfields, which makes it the right and proper place to put the No-life Man, doesn't it? Because he came from over the cornfields!"

Sam held his head in his hands. "No-one's ever come from over the cornfields! Remember Reggie Run and how they all tried to escape along the path blown by the wind? Look what happened to them!"

But no matter how outrageous were Rasper's claims, no-one on the Assembly had the courage to dispute them. Instead they began to clap and cheer.

"Put him up on the Tower on Avenue B!" roared Horne.

"That'll be a laugh!" shouted Rory.

Pike sneezed spraying Editor Thrust three yards away, but before he could protest,' Rasper had stomped to the doors, opened them wide and was leading the Assembly out. They were going to collect the No-Life Man from the Hospital right there and then!

"Send out runners!" shouted Rasper pompously.

"Prepare the Tower for the No-Life Man!" yelled Horne, who always seemed to know exactly what Rasper wanted.

"The Assembly's coming!" someone else hollered.

And they all trooped out leaving Sam and Fortuna no option but to follow. By the time Old Pen had eased himself up from his seat, they'd all gone.

SAVED BY RAGS

Outside the Town Hall door a huge crowd seemed to have gathered from nowhere. And they were all applauding Rasper as he stood there at the top of the steps with his hands raised.

"Where did they all come from?" asked Sam, amazed.

"They knew this was going to happen," said Fortuna.

"How?"

"Rasper must have organised the whole thing before he told the Assembly," said Fortuna half admiringly. "Look, he's even got the band here as well."

And there they were, marching across the Green with the buttons on their uniforms shining and their brass instruments gleaming in the sun. They followed smartly as Rasper turned in the direction of the Hospital and led the Assembly Members across the Green. The crash of the drums and the blast of the trumpets made them all feel very superior. Pike's nose had stopped running for the first time all day and he stuck it in the air. Henry Horne had his head right back and his great mouth open in a lippy grin, and Editor Thrust was trying to look important by making notes in his notebook as he walked. Sam and Fortuna followed on behind as Pen huffed and puffed, trying to keep up.

And as if the band and the Assembly weren't enough, brightly painted banners on long poles began to appear amongst the crowd, reading, *LONG LIVE THE NO-LIFE MAN!* and *RASPER OUR HERO!*

"Banners as well! He's even got banners!" gasped Fortuna.

The band played, and as the crowd marched, more came swarming across the Green to join them. It didn't take long for the whole procession to arrive outside the Hospital.

Immediately the chant went up, started by Horne and Bill Rory, "We want the No-Life Man! "Give us the No-Life Man!" Every time they said it, they thrust their fists into the air as if they were punching it.

Nurse Pine came out through the main hospital doors, saw the assembled crowd, the banners and the band, and immediately panicked. She went even brighter red than usual. "What? What do you want?"

"The No-Life Man!"

"The doctors are out on a case," she wailed.

"On the authority of the Town Assembly we demand the delivery of the No-Life Man!" Rasper roared at the unfortunate Nurse.

"Well you can have him and welcome!" she said shakily, "He only stinks the place out anyway!"

"Well take him now," shouted Rasper, "Get him!"

Four men from Awkward Corner ran up from behind him with a cart that up to now had been hidden in the crowd. It was painted gold and decorated with a red cloth. And had obviously been made to carry the No-Life Man.

"Now we know that he definitely planned the whole thing." said Sam.

"Exactly. You don't just happen to find gold carts lying around, do you?" said Fortuna. "He's making fools of all of us." But there was still that thoughtful, half admiring tone to her voice. She was watching Rasper carefully. It seemed that the bigger the lie you told, the more likely it was that people believed you.

"I wish Alice was here," said Sam half to himself as he looked around.

"What for? She'd only be dashing off again on some mad scheme or other," said Fortuna.

As the men went in though the Hospital doors, Pike, who was by now enjoying himself, turned to the leader of the band and said, "Play something solemn."

The band struck up the Thistown anthem, which was not quite what Pike meant, but Rasper nodded in approval.

"Good idea, Pike," he whispered, "Now they all know how important this No-Life Man is."

Pike looked pleased with himself.

There was a cheer. The crowd could see the men carrying the table with the No-Life Man on it through the Hospital corridor back towards them. The band began to play louder as the men came through the front doors. Everybody craned forward to see, but the No-Life Man was still covered in a sheet.

"Let's have a look at him!" yelled someone.

"When he's on top of the Tower," yelled Rasper, quietening them, "You should only look at him when he's on high!" Then he turned to the men carrying him, and said, "Put him on the cart."

The men gently lifted the No-Life Man still covered in his sheet, and laid him carefully on the red cloth of the cart. Then they quickly took up their positions ready to pull it away.

The band struck up the anthem again, and Rasper yelled, "Forward!"

Then it happened. Just as the men started to pull the cart, the No-Life Man sat up! The men stopped pulling and stepped back quickly. One of them even dived under the cart.

"Aaaagghh!" yelled Pike and he fell back into the arms of Editor Thrust behind him, who dropped his notebook. The bandsmen were so startled that they played some notes and chords that nobody had ever heard before and haven't heard since.

Then there was silence. No-one knew what to do. Everyone just stood rooted to the spot. The No-Life Man just seemed to be sitting there, doing nothing. Then suddenly a bulge appeared under the sheet. The No-Life Man seemed to be moving his hand up towards his head.

"It's a sign!" said someone.

"He's speaking to us!" quaked Pike, his voice hoarse with fear.

The No-Life Man didn't move again. His hand stayed by his face.

Sam and Fortuna were just as shocked as everybody else. The last time they'd seen the No-Life Man, he was stretched out on a table and was stinking and so stiff that any movement at all, let alone sitting up, would have been completely impossible. They watched with their mouths open as Rasper slowly approached the cart, and with a shaking hand reached for the corner of the sheet. He took hold of it between two fingers, breathed in deeply, and then whipped it high in the air. And they saw.

Sitting on the cart, half asleep and with his finger up his nose was Detective Sergeant Flouncy Willis dressed only in his underpants. He didn't notice the crowd for a second, but then slowly looked round with his eyes bulging. His mouth fell open. It was clear he had no idea where he was.

"What are you doing there?" shouted Rasper.

Willis jumped about a foot in the air. "I...I don't know."

"What do you mean, you don't know, you fat idiot! What have you done with the No-Life Man?" Rasper was in a state of fury. He'd planned the crowd, the banners and the band, and now for all his pains, all he was left with was a silly flabby detective with his finger up his nose. "Where is he?" he roared.

Willis was shaking. "I don't know, sorry. All I remember is last night I was at the People's cafe celebrating your great speech. And I..."

"You drank to much, didn't you?" Henry Horne leered.

"He was drunk!" Someone in the crowd pointed his finger at Willis. "Calls himself a detective and he can't even discover what he did himself!"

It was getting ugly and Willis was feeling very vulnerable half naked on the cart. "I think I walked home with Doctor Slice. " he suddenly remembered. " Oh I don't know!" he wailed. He was very scared by now. And who wouldn't have been, sitting in in his underpants, with half the town staring at him? Rasper was about to completely lose his temper when Nurse Pine ran out of the Hospital.

"Where is he? You tell us! Where's the No-Life Man?" yelled Rasper.

"He's gone!" said Pine. "He's nowhere to be seen."

Rasper kicked the cart with his iron leg he was so furious. He couldn't believe this was happening. Everything had been going so well, but now a few in the crowd were beginning to laugh, and he knew that if they saw him looking foolish, even for a minute, then they'd lose all faith in him.

"We must search!" he shouted, "Send out search parties!"

But before anybody could move there came the sound of a young high-pitched voice, "Help! Help! Come quick!"

And from out of the crowd came an eight year old boy called Rags, who used to hang around Awkward Corner. He was one of the runners that Rasper had sent to the Tower to tell them to prepare for the No-Life Man. On his way back he'd taken a shortcut round the Edge, and that's when he'd seen it.

"There's somebody in the Cornfields!" he shouted, his eyes wide with fear. "He's just lying there asleep and he hasn't disappeared."

"Has he got a striped shirt and blue trousers?" asked Nurse Pine catching on quicker than usual.

"Yes!" shouted Rags.

"Then that's him." said Nurse Pine triumphantly.

"The No-Life Man." said Rasper, thinking quickly. He turned back to the crowd. "Did you hear what Rags said? The No-Life Man is in the corn! And he hasn't disappeared! Didn't I tell you how different he was? Didn't I tell you how special he was? And now I'll tell you something else! If he hasn't disappeared then that means he knows about the corn, doesn't he? *Maybe he knows how to cross the corn!* Didn't I tell you he had a message for us?" He began to laugh and shout at the same time as he stomped his way through the crowd. "Didn't I tell you?"

The crowd gasped. The No-Life Man knew how to cross the corn! They weren't entirely sure of how, but it seemed that Rasper had been right all along! The No-Life Man was changing Thistown. Many of them slapped Rasper's back in congratulation as he pushed his way through them, leaving poor old Willis in his underpants on the cart, like a baby in a pram.

"Make way for Rasper!"

"Make way!"

Even Sam and Fortuna were amazed. A man in the corn who hadn't disappeared! It was too incredible for words. Could Rasper have really been right from the beginning? Sam couldn't believe it. And Fortuna didn't want to. But they followed the crowd up Avenue B to the Edge all the same. It seemed as if Rasper had been saved by a boy called Rags. Later he'd joke about it. "From Rags to riches!" he'd say, then he'd roar with laughter.

UNDISAPPEARED

The news spread like wildfire and the crowd were joined by hundreds more who swarmed onto Avenue B from every Circle intersection. They were noisy and very excited. Perhaps the No-Life Man was a messenger, after all.

Even Sam was beginning to be convinced. "Well obviously he can move," he said as he walked quickly with Fortuna. "How else did he manage to get himself from the Hospital to the cornfields?"

Fortuna just pursed her lips and followed. She didn't know what to make of any of it and until she did was going to keep her mouth shut. Soon the procession with Rasper in the lead arrived at the old Tower. The huge crowd immediately fanned out along the Edge and there, just as Rags had said, was the No-Life Man. He lay on his back about six feet into the corn.

"He looks the same as he did in the Hospital," said Fortuna having fought through the crowd for a better view.

"He's still got the same horrible grin," said Sam, joining her.

"His skin though, Yuck!" Fortuna turned away. The No-Life Man's face was turning brown and starting to crack. And he stank worse than ever. There wasn't a person near him who wasn't holding their nose.

Rasper, Henry Horne and their followers pushed the crowd back.

"We must get him out," Rasper shouted. "We must get him up onto the Tower."

"Get him up into the Tower!" yelled Henry Horne.

And several people ran around purposefully, but the truth was that nobody really knew what to do.

"Maybe the corn don't disappear you no more!" said somebody, but no-one was prepared to risk finding out by walking into the corn.

"You could try pulling him out with a pole," said Sam suddenly.

"What are you helping him for?" hissed Fortuna.

"Yes. Good idea! Pull him out with a pole," said Rasper. "Even members of the old Assembly have good ideas every now and again."

There was some laughter at Sam's expense, but every-body was too excited to take much notice of him then. They waited as two men ran to a nearby workshop and came back with two long wooden poles with hooks on the end.

"Right, one of you hook his head, and the other his feet," ordered Rasper.

The two men lowered the poles into the corn, then pulled them up. The hooks had disappeared. There was a groan from the crowd. Nothing had changed. Everything that went into the corn, disappeared. Except, of course, the No-Life Man. He stayed, with his crooked face leering up at them.

"It's very interesting isn't it?"

Sam turned quickly to see Alice standing close behind him.

"Where've you been?" he almost shouted, "Can't you see what's happening?"

"Oh I know all about that. I knew all about that last night."

Now Fortuna turned back as well, "You knew about it last night? How?"

"Ssshh!" Alice put her finger to her lips and led them away to the back of the crowd.

"Why are you always going off and doing things and not letting me know?" said Sam.

"Sam..."

"I get worried about you, you know!"

"Will you just let me tell you what happened?" Alice asked patiently.

"Go on," said Fortuna, desperately hoping for something that would prove that Rasper hadn't been right all along.

Alice carried on quietly, "You see when we put him in the corn, we thought he would disappear too."

"You put him in the corn!" gasped Fortuna.

"Why?" Sam asked.

Alice watched as she saw two men going towards the Edge with ropes to loop around the No-Life Man. "That won't do any good. The rope will only disappear too."

"Will you tell us what happened, please?" Sam was getting angry with her.

"Let's walk," she said and they turned away down Avenue B. "When I left you in the middle of Rasper's speech last night, I found Stitch and Slice on the Green and explained it to them."

"Explained what?" asked Sam.

"The same as I explained to you yesterday at the Hospital. The only way to get rid of the No-Life Man was to throw him in the corn. At least I thought that was the only way, because it would stop Rasper, and how could he use a No-Life Man that had disappeared?"

"So you and the doctors took him to the corn?" said Fortuna.

"Yes, on a Hospital trolley. And we threw him in. It really stunk I can tell you."

"But he didn't disappear, did he?" said Sam.

"No," said Alice sadly.

"And Detective Willis?" Sam asked, "How did he get into the Hospital?"

"Slice found him staggering along the road, dead drunk after he'd come out of The People's Cafe," said Alice "So we put him on the empty trolley and wheeled him to the Hospital for a good sleep. And we put the sheet over him so that Nurse Pine would think he was the No-Life Man."

"And he woke up facing the whole town in his underpants!" Said Sam, laughing for the first time that day.

"How?" asked Alice not knowing what had happened outside the Hospital.

They told her and she laughed too, but not for long. Just at that moment Henry Horne ran past them on the Avenue, shouting at the top of his voice, "Meeting on the

Green Tonight! Everyone must attend! Rasper says so! Everyone must attend!"

"Everyone *must* attend? *Rasper says so?* Who does he think he is?" said Fortuna, getting angry all over again.

"What you did Alice, has helped Rasper," said Sam.

"That's right," said Fortuna, "He was just going to put the No-Life Man up on the Tower where he would have just stunk the place out. And what could he say about that?"

"But you put him in the corn," said Sam.

"And he hasn't disappeared," said Fortuna.

"And so now Rasper can say that the No-Life Man really is special."

"And now he's holding another meeting."

"Sorry," said Alice.

"Just ask me before you do anything else, will you?" said Sam.

"How would you have known that he wouldn't have disappeared?" asked Alice angrily.

"I'd have thought about it at least!"

"But you couldn't have *known!*"

"I might have done...."

"How....?"

And so they argued all the way up Avenue B as the No-Life Man lay rotting in the corn and Fortuna went quiet as she thought some more about Rasper and how he was making all this happen.

THE FRIENDS

Miriam was upset. "It was so horrible," she said, tears filling her huge grey eyes.

She was sitting with Alice, Sam, Fortuna and Jack (Jumping Jack) Juniper on the Green. Jumping Jack was a black boy; a thin streak of amazing, flashing, leaping energy and a mass of thick hair that stuck straight up from his head. He and Miriam had both been at the the Edge to see the No-Life Man and they'd both witnessed the terrible accident that had followed.

"See, Rasper couldn't get the No-Life man out of the corn," said Jack.

"He was being very frustrated," added Miriam in her husky voice.

"So he got all the men from Workshop Way, you know, to build this wooden platform out over the corn where the No-Life Man was lying," explained Jack, "And then two other men, you know, were put up there to like spear him with these sharp sticks."

"But the platform broke down," said Miriam.

"Because they'd made it all too quick, see?"

"And they fell...." Miriam didn't want to go on.

"They went straight into the corn, whoosh" said Jack as if he'd known what was going to happen all the time.

"And so they disappeared," added Miriam sadly.

They were quiet for a moment. Perhaps occasionally someone had gone too close to the corn and lost a foot or a hand, or there were odd times when a drunk had fallen in and disappeared, but to lose two men at the same time was almost unheard of, and it upset them.

"Who were these men?" asked Sam.

"One was Peter Fry and the other one was Walton Wall. They both worked on the Workshop Way." said Miriam with tears in her eyes. "I knew Mr Walton. He lived near me and gave me herbs for my teas. Old Croker said, 'Let's put a plaque up in their memory', but Rasper wasn't even listening."

"Rasper! Rasper! Rasper!" hissed Fortuna. "It's all I ever hear! It's always Rasper, isn't it? It was his fault that they were up in the tower in the first place!"

"So what did he do when Peter and Walt disappeared?" asked Alice. She felt as sad as Miriam did.

" He just walked up and down. No-one knew what to say, they were too shocked." said Miriam.

"Then he shouted, it's the power of the No-Life Man!" said Jack.

"It was nothing to do with the No-Life Man," said Sam, "He didn't build the tower did he?"

"According to Rasper, everything is to do with the No-Life Man," said Fortuna.

"Yeah, that's what he said." said Jack, "He said, this No-Life Man will give us everything! And so then he told Pike and Henry Horne to get everybody onto the Green tonight."

"Did he ask the New Assembly for permission?" asked Sam.

"Of course he didn't," spat Fortuna.

"Then the meeting is illegal," Sam shook his head.

"Will you shut up!" Fortuna was getting really angry now. "Everything Rasper does is *illegal*. We know that already!"

"Rasper don't run Thistown!" shouted Jack jumping up angrily. "He never has done and he never will! There are Peter Fry and Walter Wall disappeared because of him, you know!"

Miriam pointed at the Town Hall, as if they all knew that Rasper would be inside. "The last thing he said was this, all we needed was the No-Life Man. And no-one else."

"And everyone else said, 'Yes, oh yes! Yes, please!' They are so retarded!" Jack was walking around angrily under the trees.

He was right. Certainly all of Raspers' followers from Awkward Corner seemed to have completely lost their heads. Up to now they'd seemed harmless enough, but with the rise of Rasper they'd quickly become peculiar and nasty, and they'd been around the town all afternoon, bullying everyone they met into coming to the meeting on the Green that evening.

"I think it's about time we did something," said Alice.

"What can we do?" moaned Miriam. "The whole town is on his side."

"That's because they're listening to what he tells them," said Alice. Sam could see by the look in her eyes that she had thought of something.

"So how are we supposed to stop them doing that? Fortuna sneered.

"Maybe we don't," said Alice, and she grinned. "Sam do you know anything about microphones?"

Sam nodded slowly, "Yes. Probably."

"Come closer," Alice huddled the rest of them together and they began to whisper. There was some arguement, but finally they all agreed what they were going to do. After a long time they slipped away, avoiding Rasper's bullies who had by now managed to turn the disappearance of Peter Fry and Walt Wall into the best thing that had ever happened to Thistown.

Sam went quickly across to Avenue R, and walked up it to his house on the Fifth Circle. After an of hour rooting through mounds of cardboard and piles of wood and boxes full of old tin cans he'd found enough to make a start on what they needed. But as he worked cutting the card and bending the tin around the shaped wooden frames, there was one question on his mind that wouldn't go away. Why had Pete and Walt disappeared in the corn, and the No-Life Man hadn't?

ON THE GREEN AGAIN

The crowd began to assemble on the Green. Around the edge stood Bill Rory and a whole gang from Awkward Corner. They were all intently watching the crowd, as if they were looking out for anyone who might disagree with them or Rasper. And what was worse, the Chief of Police seemed to be asking his men to do the same thing. Detective Willis, who'd recovered from what he'd called his underpant mortification outside the hospital by cringing and crawling to Henry Horne was already writing a name in his notebook to prove that he was a true Rasperite.

"Rasperite! They call themselves Rasperite? What kind of name is that? It sounds so...so...stupid!" Miriam was standing on the Green with Sam as the crowd packed in around them.

"It's so they can all crawl to him," said Sam as he looked around.

If anything this occasion was more festive than the last which worried him. If Rasper could get everyone to enjoy themselves he was half way to persuading them. The band was already playing, lights had been festooned around the trees, and huge banners had been strung up from the windows of the buildings around the Green. There was the usual *Long live the No-Life Man'* with others on the same theme *'The No-Life Man will save us'* and *'Follow the No-Life Man."*

"How can you follow someone who's lying rotting in the corn?" Miriam wanted to know.

"And how can you argue against someone who doesn't make sense?" said Sam. This was what really depressed him. Steady old Sam who would always think carefully abut everything had suddenly found himself with no idea what to say or do about Rasper, except maybe shout and scream and jump around in a stupid rage. And that was something that old sensible Sam could never do. He looked around the Green as if filled up.

"Look!" said Miriam. "They've even got pictures of him now!"

Sam couldn't believe it. All around them people were producing placards and even pictures that were hero-worshipping Rasper. *'Rasperites Rise!'* was everywhere and there were even a few *'Rasper Rules!'*

"It gets more incredible every second," said Sam as he looked around for Alice. He'd spent the afternoon making the three loud hailers she'd wanted. She'd tested them and had laughed delightedly as her voice had boomed out along Avenue W near her house.

"What are you going to do with them?" Sam had asked.

"You'll see!" said Alice. Then she'd run off to find Fortuna. And as usual hadn't come back.

"I thought they were going to stand all along the Green and shout things out through them," said Miriam.

"So did I," said Sam, "but you know Alice. She's probably thought of something else and hasn't bothered to mention it to us."

"Perhaps she didn't like the police." Miriam was watching as Detective Willis wrote something else in his notebook. "What's he writing down so much anyway?"

"Probably our names." Sam was getting even more depressed. He had a feeling that this was all going to go wrong. And where was Alice?

"She will be alright," it was as if Miriam could read his mind. "Don't worry." She smiled her beautiful smile and took his hand.

A MAYOR

The Town Hall clock struck eight and the New Town Assembly slowly filed out onto the balcony led by Henry Horne with Bill Rory at the back, as if he was making sure that none of them would run away. As they stepped into the light from the huge lanterns that had been hung from the roof, the whole crowd could see that they all wore bright blue uniforms! They gasped. Up until now the only sign that someone was an Assembly Member had been a small badge they wore on their lapel. No-one wanted Assembly members to think themselves more important than they were, (which was just to represent the wishes of the people and nothing else), and they certainly didn't need uniforms to prove anything!

"They're in uniforms!" said Sam "I don't believe it."

"And what a horrible kind of blue too," sighed Miriam.

"Where's Pike?" Sam peered up at the lanterns. "Oh no!"

There was another blast from the trumpets, the doors at the back of the balcony opened and a delighted Pike came out with his nose in the air. He had a coat of shiny blue and was wearing a hat made of blue feathers.

"What's that!" exclaimed Miriam, her eyes bulging.

Pike approached the microphone as some of the crowd laughed into their hands at his ridiculous hat. "My people," he shouted in his high voice.

"*My* People! We're not *his* People! Who does he think is!" Sam was furious by now, but Miriam gave him a nudge. Detective Willis and the Chief of Police were standing nearby watching them closely.

"Quiet, Sam."

"Oh where's Alice?" moaned Sam. "They were supposed to be using the loud hailers now to stop all this.

Pike went on, "Today the great Rasper has appointed me Mayor of Thistown!"

"Mayor! We've never had a mayor!" said Sam.

"Well we've got one again now," said Miriam sadly.

"That's just so Pike will do everything Rasper wants him to!" They'd never leaders of any kind, let alone a mayor. The Head of the Assembly was only there to make sure that everyone didn't speak at the same time, he certainly didn't have any more power than anyone else, and he definitely wasn't a mayor who wore a stupid hat which was a foot high and made of blue feathers!

Pike made a little bow towards Rasper, "I want to say I am privileged. Thank you, Rasper. Only you would have the great wisdom to create the office of Mayor and to give myself and the Town Assembly uniforms. It's a great privilege to wear them. People of Thistown, I ask you to show your appreciation for the great man himself! *Ronald Rasper!*"

He applauded wildly, the Assembly Members behind him began to do the same thing, and Awkward Corner

Rasperites on the Green below started to shout and cheer. Soon most of the rest of the crowd and all the police officers were cheering as well.

But Sam noticed there was beginning to be a hesitancy in the crowd as Rasper came forward to the microphone. They were obviously not too sure about all this. Now they had a Mayor that they probably didn't want, and Assembly Members who'd been chosen by Rasper, and in blue uniforms too. This wasn't the Thistown they knew. Maybe there was hope yet, Sam thought.

Rasper was in his usual black trousers and grubby white shirt. It was as if he felt he was too important to wear a uniform, or he was trying to convince everybody that he was still just ordinary old Rasper. He raised his arms and began to speak. "My friends!" he roared into the microphone. "My people of Thistown...!"

And then suddenly he was talking but no sound was coming out of the speakers that had been placed round the Green. His microphone had gone dead. There was confusion as several of the Browncoat Boys went to try and fix it. But hardly had they started when the lights in the banqueting rooms above the balcony came on. Three big windows opened and there was Alice, Fortuna, and Jumping Jack Juniper each holding one of Sam's home made loud hailers.

REVOLUTION

"There they are!" shouted Miriam. "Above the balcony, look!" Miriam pointed up as Fortuna shouted into her loud hailer,*"Don't listen to Rasper!"*

"He'll only give you lies!" yelled Jack.

It was difficult to see the three of them clearly because the light behind them in the banqueting rooms was so bright. Maybe because of this, the crowd pushed forward to hear what they had to say.

"Rasper just wants to take over!" shouted Alice.

Bill Rory and all the police officers ran quickly from the Green towards the Town Hall. Up above on the balcony Henry Horne and several other Rasperites ran to the doors and disappeared into the building behind. Sam knew exactly where they were going. They were running towards the stairs in the Town Hall that led up to his friends in the rooms above.

"He only wants power for himself!" Fortuna shouted.

Rasper and Pike, on the balcony below with their microphone switched off, could only look up as they went on.

"He doesn't have the right to make a Mayor!" shouted Alice through her loud hailer.

"Only the people have that right!" This was Fortuna.

"And the people is us!" yelled Miriam below on the Green. She turned to those around her. "Yes, it's us. There's no need to be scared to say so!"

Some of the crowd around her agreed and shouted out too, "We are the people, not Rasper!"

"We don't want you to agree with us, we want you to decide for yourselves!" Alice shouted back down to them.

"And get rid of Rasper!" This was Fortuna again. *"Get rid of him!"*

"Before he destroys our town!" yelled Alice.

"Before he.....! "Jack tried to say something.

And then suddenly Sam, to his horror, saw his friends being surrounded by blue uniformed Rasperites led by Henry Horne and Bill Rory. Their loud hailers were pulled out of their hands as they were dragged back from the windows. Then the lights in the banqueting rooms went out and those on the Green couldn't see what was happening.

"Oh, no!" said Sam. "Oh no."

Someone shouted, "What's going on?" The crowd too were uneasy. They didn't know what to make of the abrupt disappearance of the young people from the windows. They watched silently as the Browncoat Boys repaired Rasper's microphone. Finally he stepped forward on the balcony as Percy Pike, Henry Horne, Bill Rory and the other Assembly members lined up again behind him in a solid wall of blue.

"Now you've seen our enemies!" Rasper shouted angrily. The microphone seemed twice as loud. Perhaps one of the Browncoat Boys had turned it up, or more likely Rasper himself. "Now you've heard their lies!"

Horne and Bill Rory and then Pike started to shout their support and clap Rasper, urging the crowd to do the same.

"They say, I only want power for myself!" Rasper yelled. "Did I bring the No-Life Man to Thistown? No, I didn't! Did I try and cover up his message? No, I didn't! Who did? The Old Assembly, that's who! They wanted to keep the No-Life Man as their secret! Well, I showed him to you! I broke up this corrupt Old Assembly! And I have given the New Assembly uniforms so that they can never be secret again!"

Pike and the New Assembly all shouted their approval, although in Pike's case it was more like a whine. To Sam's dismay, some in the crowd down below were beginning to applaud Rasper again.

Rasper flung his hands wide. "And listen to me, my people, let me prove to you that I don't want power for myself! I have something much better than power! I have a dream! I have had a dream for the good of Thistown! Shall I tell you this dream?"

"Yes!!" shouted Horne and the others on the balcony.

Most of the crowd remained quiet. But it's a fact that Thistonians liked dreams and they were waiting to hear Rasper's.

"Listen to my dream." Rasper said in a dramatic whisper. He wrapped his arms across his chest, closed his eyes and his voice became deep and hypnotic. "In my dream there was a wonderful brightness in the sky. It was a golden glow above the corn which moved slowly further and further away over the fields until finally it seemed as if it was on the other side of the corn. This light became so bright I could I hardly bring myself to look into it. Then I began to see a strange dark shape in the middle of it. This shape slowly became bigger and bigger. And as the light got even brighter, the shape grew, and grew, and finally I could see what this shape was. It was the No-Life Man! He became even bigger until he was so vast that he had blocked out the light!"

Some of the crowd gasped.

"He had come to me in my dream!" said Rasper. "But most importantly. He had come to me from *the other side of the corn!*"

There were excited murmurs and mutterings in the crowd. Many of them believed that all dreams were true.

Rasper slowly raised his arms. "And he spoke, The No-Life Man spoke to me!" The crowd waited, "He told me that he would show us the way over the corn!" He stopped and looked out over the crowd. "But only if we build." There was absolute silence, no-one moved. "I said to the No-Life Man. Oh show me what to build." Rasper's voice was getting more and more powerful, "And then I saw it.

It stood high and shining. It was the most magnificent and beautiful thing I had ever seen. It was a huge golden temple! And it had been made by us! It was a *Great Hall!*"

"A Great Hall." Even Henry Horne could only look at Bill Rory in amazement.

"A Great Hall by the Corn. *A Great Hall on the Edge!*"

"A Great Hall on the Edge." the idea was passed from one person to another in the throng below. "Built by us." The excitement in the crowd was rising.

"We've never had a great hall in Thistown!" said Rasper. "Why not? Because nothing has ever been important enough to make us build one. But now there is, isn't there?" He didn't have to say it, everyone knew what he was talking about.

"The No-Life Man!" The crowd shouted as one.

"A Great Hall on the Edge where we can look out over the *No-Life Man!"* Rasper roared.

"The No-Life Man!" the crowd roared back.

"He has come to me in my dreams and he will come to me again, and he will show us what to do!" Rasper shouted. "He will lead us if we build this Great Hall!"

"Build the Hall! Build the Hall!" The crowd began to chant led by Rasperites.

"Build the Hall and we'll find the way over the Corn!" Rasper roared.

The crowd cheered and cheered. Some of them even danced.

Sam moved away from them to the edge of the Green. He didn't know what to think. Thistown had been the same for hundreds of years and no-one had ever crossed the cornfields, but now apparently a Man with No Life was going to tell them all how to do it if they built a Great Hall. It all seemed completely crazy, but the people on the Green were dancing and shouting as if it was the simplest and most obvious thing they'd ever heard. He turned away to see Miriam looking up at Rasper with tears in her eyes.

"Miri?" Sam couldn't believe that she'd been taken in by him too.

"I have never hated anyone more than I hate Rasper," she said.

"It's crazy, it's crazy. Everything is crazy."

"I know," she said. "And there's nothing we can do."

"I'm going to find Alice," said Sam.

"They have taken her. They have taken all of them." Miriam was crying now.

"I'll find them." Sam went off through the crowd. Miriam didn't try to stop him. She thought of her brave friends trying to speak the truth through their loud hailers from the banqueting rooms. No-one had listened. And never again would anyone in Thistown be able to say what they thought. She looked around the crowd. She saw the police making notes and she knew that from then on there would always be someone watching them and reporting what they saw back to the Rasperites.

MISSING

Sam didn't find Alice, or Fortuna, or Jack Juniper.

By the time he got to the Town Hall, the crowd round the huge doors was too dense for him to get through. He could hear the Rasperites celebrating inside and many of those out on the Green were beginning to pass beer bottles around. He crept round the back of the hall to see if he could find another way in. He couldn't, and the windows were too high for him to look through. Finally he climbed a tree at the back of the hall. As he was halfway up he thought he heard a voice he recognised. He nearly fell out of the tree as he strained to hear. It went quiet again. He climbed a bit more and was sure he heard, "Hey you! Get off me!"

It was Jack! Sam climbed higher until he was level with the banqueting room windows on the top floor of the Town Hall. There was a small chink of light coming through the thick curtains which had been pulled closed. He leaned as far out of the tree as he dared. It was difficult because the branches were much thinner at the top. He climbed a little further and craned his neck until he could see through the chink. There was Alice! She was standing calmly by a door as Bill Rory held her arm. They were watching as two blue-uniformed Rasperites struggled with Jack.

Sam heard Alice say, or at least he thought he heard her say, "Don't, Jack. Don't fight them, it's not worth it."

Whatever it was that she said, Jack calmed down and was led from the room. Then Sam saw Fortuna being led out. Her head was high and proud and she went out saying nothing. The last to go was Alice. Sam wanted to desperately to jump from the tree, smash through the window and pull her away from the Rasperites who held her. As she went, she suddenly turned and looked directly towards the window. Sam waved as crazily as he could. Alice stared at the window and he couldn't make out whether she could see him or not. Then she pointed down, or at least Sam thought she did, because at that moment he slipped and fell at least twenty feet down through the tree, only grabbing at a thicker branch at the last minute to save himself. Was Alice only pointing down to tell him to get out of the tree? If that was true, then he'd certainly done as he was told. He dropped down the last few feet to the ground and immediately saw Detective Sergeant Willis standing by the corner of the Town Hall.

"Flouncy, what are they doing to them?" Sam asked desperately.

"Flouncy? What do you mean, Flouncy, I am Sergeant Willis to you!"

"What's the matter with you?" Sam couldn't help himself, "Can't you see what they're doing?"

"What *who* are doing?" Flouncy turned so he was facing Sam. His fat face wobbled as he spat, "Are you talking about the great Rasper?"

"Yes!" said Sam. Then he said, "No." And looked away. He was still shaking from his fall from the tree, and from the sight of his friends being held by the Rasperites.

"I hope not," said Willis, rocking slightly and sneering threateningly. Sam could see he was drunk. "Because if you are, you can go to the same place as them."

"Where's that?" Sam tried to be as calm as possible.

"That's official Rasperite business."

"But could you? I mean, tell me, because...." Sam didn't finish.

"You go sticking your nose into things that don't concern you!" Flouncy poked a beer bottle at him. "And you'll get it!"

"Why would I get it? What have I done?"

"You're asking too many questions. And I don't like it. Now get lost or I'll..." Flouncy staggered backwards and then suddenly drunkenly walked away as if he couldn't remember why he was there in the first place.

Sam was left standing in the dark shadow of the Town Hall and decided that the best thing to do was wait and see where they took his friends later. He guessed that at some time they'd probably be led over to the police station on the First Circle and Avenue T.

He found a dark corner and sat and waited. The crowd on the Green finally went home singing the praises of Rasper until the Avenues echoed. After another hour or two the celebrations inside the Hall stopped and all the lights went out. And still no-one came out. Perhaps they'd all just fallen asleep in the Assembly chamber, or maybe Rasper and his cronies had decided to move in! He wouldn't put it past them.

He waited all night and saw nothing. And then he waited some more until nine o'clock in the morning and still the great doors hadn't opened. He had half a mind to go and bang on them and demand that he be allowed to speak to Alice, but he knew it wouldn't do any of them much good for him to be arrested as well. He was cold and lonely and needed someone to talk to. He began the long walk to Avenue U and the Thirtieth Circle.

Miriam had been so worried, she hadn't slept either. She'd tried all the sleep remedies she knew but nothing would keep her eyes closed for longer than a minute or two. She sat hollow eyed across the low table from a weary Sam as he sat sipping a cup of tea.

"What shall we do, Miri?" he asked forlornly. "I know it's no good asking any Rasperite. Flouncy Willis…"

"Mr Underpants Willis," said Miriam scornfully.

"Whatever he is, he'd have arrested me himself last night if he hadn't been drunk. He walked away and fell over instead."

"What about the Chief of Police?" asked Miriam. "We could go to the police station and ask him."

"He won't help?"

"If you can't ask the police, who can you ask?"

Miri was right. What else was there? Sam reluctantly agreed. "Alright," he said. "We can try the Chief."

He went to get up, but the sleepless night and the long walk had exhausted him and he sat back down again onto his chair.

"Not yet," said Miriam gently, "It is not good to undertake a journey with a weary soul."

"Please, Miri." Sam didn't want any of her philosophising just now.

"Lie on my couch and I'll mix up something for you."

"Miri…" He tried again to push himself up from the table, but it was no good, he was too tired. Miriam smiled and took his hand. She led him over to the sofa and gently pushed him back down into the soft silk cushions. Soon there was a sweet and comforting scent wafting over him.

"Breath in deeply," she said as she mixed up more herbs. "And close your eyes."

He did as he was told, laid his head back, and began to feel his eyelids getting heavier. Hardly before he knew it, he was asleep and dreaming of the cornfields waving in the sun as if they were inviting him to come in and disappear forever. There was a part of him that wanted to it, and just as he was about to walk towards them he woke up with a start to find Miriam standing over him holding her coat.

"How long have I been asleep?"

"For one hour," said Miriam with a smile.

He sat up quickly, he could feel that the tiredness had gone from his legs and the coldness from his bones. He said, "The Chief of Police, weren't we…?."

She went to the door, "What are you waiting for, Mr Samson?"

He got up and followed her out onto Avenue U. It was a long walk back to the Green, but whatever it was that she had mixed for him had put the spring back in his step, and in just over an hour they were standing outside the police station.

THE CHIEF OF POLICE

And in just over two hours they were still standing at the counter.

"The Chief of Police will see you now," the Sergeant finally said officiously, although he doesn't like to be disturbed in his tea break."

"Has he been having a tea break since we got here!?" said Sam losing his patience.

"Quiet you. Be grateful he's seeing you at all. That way." And the Sergeant pointed to the stairs leading up to the Chief's office.

He was eating when they walked in. He wiped his hand across his greasy mouth and said, "I know why you're here. They were thrown out of the Town Hall, that's all I know."

"No they weren't," said Sam, "I was there watching all night."

"You'll have to ask the Rasperites. They're in charge now."

"And what about the police?" asked Sam, "Aren't they in charge anymore?"

"Isn't it wonderful about the Great Hall?" said the Chief, "I always knew something good would come out of the No-Life Man."

"Chief...." Sam persisted.

"I haven't seen them and that's that." the Chief said.

"Please, Mr..." Miriam tried to speak.

"And if you ask me, they deserve all they got!" the Chief cut her off. "They were trying to stop the meeting weren't they? And just imagine if they had! None of us would have heard the Great Dream Speech, would we? And we'd never have even *thought* about a Great Hall!"

Sam looked at him. "Is that what you really think?"

"Yes" said the Chief, "it is." But he turned away as he said it.

"Do you know where our friends are, please?" Miriam looked at him with her huge eyes.

The Chief remained turned away, and Sam thought he seemed a bit ashamed of himself.

He spread his hands, "What can I do?" he said. "What can I do?" He stuffed a sandwich in his mouth and defiantly chewed on it.

"Please, Mr."

But the Chief just chewed.

"You see, we always trusted the Police and we thought..."

The Chief carried on chewing and wouldn't look at them.

"Come on, Miri," said Sam. "He won't help us. He hasn't lost his friends, has he?"

They went sadly back down the stairs. The Sergeant on the desk didn't even look up as they passed.

"Now what do we do?" asked Sam angrily once they were outside the station and back down on the Green.

"I don't think he knew where they were anyway," said Miriam.

"He's just scared of the Rasperites like everyone else,"

"So I suppose we'll have to ask them ourselves,"

"You mean, go and talk to them?"

"Yes." Miriam was terrified at the thought.

Sam looked over at the Town Hall. The door was still locked shut. "They won't even open the door."

Miriam looked across the Green towards Awkward Corner.

"I think I know where they might be," said Miriam.

"In the People's Cafe?"

"Yes."

"Alice and Fortuna?"

"No. The Rasperites."

THE PEOPLE'S CAFE.

It didn't take them long to walk across the Green, although every step seemed to make them more nervous. When they arrived outside the People's Cafe, the door was shut and there were no lights on inside.

"I was wrong. No-one's here," said Miriam.

"Wait a minute. Why don't we see?" Sam strode up to the red door and banged hard with his fist. To his surprise the door immediately swung open, and the first person they saw was Henry Horne. He was sitting at a table with Bill Rory. They both looked hungover. Sam knew exactly how long they'd celebrated in the Town Hall the night before and could imagine how much beer they'd drunk. They must have spent the night there and come over here while he was lying asleep on Miriam's cushions. The two men had dark and angry expressions on their faces as they stared up at them standing in the doorway.

"Excuse me" Sam said.

"Who are you?" asked Rory with a sneer.

"You know who I am,"

Rory leaned towards them as if he was giving them a good look over. Sam could smell the stink of beer on his breath. Then he noticed that other Rasperites were drinking in the gloom at the back of the cafe, and the horrible thought struck him that they hadn't finished celebrating at all, and were all still drunk.

"Where are our friends?" said Sam trying not to show his fear.

"You mean the ones with the loud hailers?"

Sam wasn't sure whether he should admit it or not, but decided to stand his ground, "Yes, they're our friends. Where are they?"

"Perhaps they've been chucked in the corn?" Rory leered and several of the Rasperites in the gloom behind him started to laugh.

Miriam said, "No."

Sam went pale.

Rory roared with laughter, "Look at their faces. You'll never know, will you?"

"Shut-up you idiot!" Horne suddenly pulled Rory back. The laughter stopped. "This is a serious business." He turned to Sam. "We know you have the same ideas as your friends." His eyes narrowed. "You are enemies of Thistown."

"We are not the enemies of Thistown," said Sam indignantly. "Thistown is our town, it's where we live. How can we be its enemies?"

"You're either with us or against us," said Horne. "Which are you?"

"I'm not with or against anyone," said Sam.

"With us or against us!" Someone had shouted it from inside the cafe. It was beginning to turn ugly and Miriam wanted to go. "Sam..."

Horne suddenly grabbed her arm. "We threw your little mates out of the Town Hall last night. And that's all you need to know." He pushed her away from him.

"You threw them out? When?" asked Sam.

"As soon as we took their loud hailers away."

"No you didn't! I saw you...."

"What did you see?" asked Horne with a threatening look.

Sam had been about to say that he'd seen Jack and the others being dragged down through a door in the banqueting room, but he thought better of it.

"And where did they get the loud hailers anyway?" Horne stared straight at Sam.

"You know where they are, don't you?" Sam said, surprised at his own sudden burst of anger. "Tell me!" Horne looked as though he was going to get up and grab him, but it didn't stop Sam, "I want to know where Alice Bright is!"

Horne suddenly laughed, "Oh, you've lost your little friend, have you?"

"He's lost his little friend!" Rory jeered. And others began to laugh. Then someone threw a bottle which smashed on the door frame above Miriam's head.

"Sam! Come on, Sam!" She grabbed the back of his jacket and pulled.

"I'll be back," Sam shouted. "And I'll find them, whatever you've done with them." The last of his courage gone, he ran out of the cafe as another bottle crashed into the wall by the door.

They ran quickly up Avenue A and didn't stop running until they stopped breathless on the Green. They could still hear the laughter of the Rasperites in the cafe behind them.

"What do we do now?" said Miriam close to tears.

"I don't know," said Sam desperately. "If we go and see Rasper, it would be worse. And as for Percy Pike...." He stopped. It was hopeless.

"There's nothing that we can do! They control the whole town, Sam!"

Sam stood with his back against an old oak tree. "Thistown doesn't really want Rasper," he said, "How can they?"

"But even if that's true, they're too scared of him to do anything about it," said Miriam.

"Well, I'm not," said Sam, and then after a second he had to admit. "Yes I am." He stared down at the ground as an old copy of the Opinion blew across his feet with its **Let's Face the Facts** headline. It seemed very out of date now.

"The Opinion doesn't come out anymore," said Miriam sadly.

"But it was trying to tell the truth, wasn't it?" said Sam. "And how many people know the truth of what's happened to Alice and Fortuna and the others?"

"No-one," said Miriam. "I can bet you there'll be nothing about them in the Clarion, that's for sure."

"So why don't we use the Opinion like Alice did?" asked Sam.

"You mean make another paper?"

"Why not?"

"Will Mr Pen let us?"

"I'll bet he'll help us!" said Sam. "And even if no-one buys it, at least they could still see the headlines on the newstands!"

"We could put their pictures on the front page!"

"Like the Rasperites did to us!" said Sam excited at the thought.

It cheered them up to even think about it. Doing something, anything at all, meant they could at least still have hope.

Old Pen was asleep in his chair as they came pounding up the stairs.

"Mr Pen! Mr Pen!" They explained their idea to him. It didn't take long to persuade him. He was as worried about his 'best assistant Alice' as they were. They all worked for the rest of the day.

On the front page, Pen and Sam put the headline, *THE THISTOWN THREE* over the pictures of Alice Bright, Fortuna Mink, and Jack Juniper. Pen wrote a short article about how the three had tried to start a revolution against Rasper and had disappeared, or 'been disappeared,' as he put it. Sam wrote another article about the No-Life Man and how a man who was rotting and stank, and said nothing and couldn't even move or breathe, shouldn't be allowed to change people's lives, no matter what Rasper said.

While Sam and Pen were busy, Miriam sat scribbling by a window. Finally as Pen was telling Sam how to work the great printing presses, she stood up and said, "Perhaps you would like this too, Mr Pen? It's a kind of poem."

"This is too serious for poems, Miri," said Sam.

"Oh. I'm sorry." Miriam looked down.

"Wait a minute," said Old Pen. He could see the hurt in Miriam's eyes. "Everyone has a voice, Sam," he said gently. "What is it you want to say, Miriam?"

She held up her piece of paper. "You sometimes have letters from readers, don't you? So this is one from me."

Pen held his head up in that old editor way of his and said, "Read it to us."

Miriam cleared her throat and read out in her light, quavery voice.

Dear Mr Editor and People of Thistown.
We have lived for hundreds of years
in peace and harmony, oh yes.
We loved each other and we never got older at all.
We stayed as we are, perfect in our bodies, quiet
in our minds, and respectful of the town around us.
There was never any No-Life in Thistown before.
Now we are told that only a body that rots in
the cornfields can show us how to be,
and only a man called Ronald Rasper can hear the
words spoken by this body.
I may be a young and stupid girl, but I think,
Ronald Rasper is Bad with a capital B.
He is using the No-Life Man for himself.
Don't listen to him, please.
If you do you will destroy everything we have made.
Thistown is our town
And it's all we have.
Look after it.
Yours sincerely,
Miriam Marjorami.

She put her piece of paper on the table and sat down. Sam was silent for quite a while and then he said, "Sorry, Miri."

Old Pen picked up the paper, pushed his glasses back on his nose and read it again carefully. Then he put it down again. "Miriam Marjorami," he said in his cracked old ancient voice, "I would be very proud to put your letter into my paper."

Hardly had he spoken and hardly had Miriam's face broken into a brilliant smile than there was a crash of footsteps on the stairs. The door burst open and Rasper himself stormed into the office with Henry Horne, Bill Rory and a dozen other Rasperites.

He stuck his bearded chin out and said, "Think you're going to print a paper, do you?" He plucked Miriam's letter out of Pen's hand, "Going to print this?" He held the letter close to his nose as he looked at it. "Who's this Miriam Majami?"

"Marjorami. It's me," said Miriam quietly.

"So you think I'm bad, do you?"

"It's my opinion. I can have my opinion, please, can't I?"

"No *you can't!*"" roared Rasper.

"So who can?" said Sam defiantly, taking heart from Miriam's courage. "Just you?"

"That's right," said Rasper. "Just me. Do you think I don't know what's going on in my own town?"

"You're town? It's not your town!" Sam said angrily.

"We saw you!" laughed Rasper. "We saw you run over the Green and up here! Everyone tells me everything! And you want to know why? Because they're *my people!*

and it's *my town!*" He glared round at them. "And now we'll show you what we do to our enemies." He nodded to Horne and the other Rasperites. They produced hammers and crowbars from behind their backs

"What are you waiting for?" said Rasper.

They ran into the printshop with a whoop of delight and brought the hammers and iron bars crashing down on the printing presses, breaking them up.

Old Pen was forced to watch with tears in his eyes as they began to smash up the machinery that had printed his newspaper for hundreds of years. "What for? Why, oh why?" was all he could say as he sat slowly at his desk.

"Because you defied me," gloated Rasper as Horne slammed his crowbar into a rack of letters set up to print the next edition. Sam watched in horror as their typeset headline, ***THE THISTOWN THREE*** was smashed and the letters scattered all over the floor. Miriam stood by the window with tears in her eyes as Rasper slowly screwed her letter into a tight ball and threw it into the piles of broken metal and shattered glass. Finally the battering stopped. The old machines were now just broken, dented hulks of no use to anyone. The Rasperites stood back, breathless, grinning and happy from the destruction.

"Well," said Pen when it was done. "Perhaps now that you have destroyed my newspaper, you could tell us where our three young friends are."

"Funnily enough," replied Rasper, "That's what I came to ask you."

"What?" said Sam with a glance at Miriam. "You mean you don't know?" His heart leapt. If Rasper didn't know then that could only mean one thing. He couldn't believe it. Had they....?

"They escaped," said Rasper. "Where'd they go?"

Sam couldn't help it. His right arm shout involuntarily into the air, and he shouted, "Yes!"

Rasper didn't have them after all!

"Where are they?" Rasper shouted.

Sam shrugged, "That's what we've been asking all day. Why do you think we were trying to bring out the paper?"

"They're lying," said Horne. "They're just trying to put us off the track."

"No," said Rasper thinking about it, "No, they're too stupid for that. Get out!" Horne tried to argue with him, but Rasper wouldn't listen. "Out! Now!" He shouted.

Horne and the others left. Rory smashed a chair with a last hammer blow as he went. As their steps echoed on the stairs, Rasper said quietly, "Look around you." They looked sadly at the smashed presses, "Now you know what we do to our enemies. If you see these three, you tell them that." And he turned and followed the others out.

Old Pen got up slowly from his chair and walked slowly through the remains of what had been his life's work. He stopped and picked up a letter O from those spread over the floor. "The Opinion," he said sadly.

"Don't worry, Mr Pen," said Sam. " If the three of them are still out there, we can do anything, including making a new newspaper." He paused for a second, "All we have to do is find them."

BELLE FELLOWS

Sam and Miriam walked all the Circles of Thistown over the next few weeks, looking for the missing three. They went into every factory on Workshop Way, they scoured the great park between the Twelfth and Thirty-fifth Circles, they trudged past every house on every Avenue. And to make matters worse, everywhere they went they were followed by a Rasperite who hoped that they would lead them to their friends. It made no difference, they found nothing. Sam began to get depressed.

The first places they'd looked had been their friend's houses. As he stood in Alice's living room he realised how much he missed her and her cheery smile. He even missed her running off on some mad idea and not telling him where she was. He missed the manic energy of Jack Juniper. And he even missed Fortuna Mink with her blazing black eyes. She was brave, he thought, even if she was so angry all the time. These were his friends, and Thistown seemed dark and unwelcoming without them. He wanted desperately to find them, but it seemed hopeless.

As they searched they sometimes passed the the corner of Avenue A and the Forty-ninth Circle where the huge stone monster of Rasper's Great Hall was slowly taking shape on the Edge. It seemed that everyone in Thistown was working on it. Two blocks of houses, and three workshops had been demolished to make space for it. When it was finished it would be easily the biggest building in Thistown. It had a huge window facing the cornfields. Inside would be a gallery hundreds of feet long for visitors to look down on the No-Life Man. He still lay in the corn, although his clothes and flesh had rotted and he was nothing but bones, whitened by the sun. Soon the bones would turn into dust and the wind would blow it away.

But even if there'd be nothing to look at they still carried on building the Great Hall. Rasper drove all the workers hard and there was no happiness in what they were doing. It was also dangerous. The outer wall was built close to the corn and already two stonemasons had fallen in and disappeared. Rasper just shrugged and told them all to work harder. He wanted the Great Hall finished in record time. Vincente Smith, Thistown's most brilliant painter had been asked to create a vast mural for the Hall's East wall. It was to be a portrait of the No-Life Man, one hundred feet high. It would be without any doubt the biggest single thing in Thistown.

"A painting of a man going rotten in the corn! Can you believe it?" said Sam to Miriam as they looked up at the scaffolding that was being erected for Vincente to climb up and begin work. They hadn't much else to do. They had walked all the way round the last Circle and found nothing. Perhaps the three had disappeared in the corn after all. Sam sighed. It was getting dark and they were tired. They turned away from the all the noise and clatter of the construction of the Great hall and walked slowly back up the gloom of Avenue B.

They stopped as they heard a terrible sound. In front of them was an opening in a wall. A group of Rasperites were pulling a donkey into a brightly lit doorway. The beast was terrified, and screaming horrible high pitched hee-haws and heaving back from the doorway with all its might, but there were too many men who pulled and pushed and finally got it inside. There was one final, spine chilling scream from the donkey and then silence.

"Oh no," said Miriam. "What have they done?"

All they could hear was the laughter of the Rasperites.

"Sam, what have they done?"

"I don't know," said Sam, "And I don't want to either." He walked quickly away, "It's hopeless," he said as the darkness enveloped them again. "If they're doing that to donkeys, what are they going to do to the rest of us?"

"What did they do to the donkey?"

Sam just shook his head.

"We're not beaten yet," said Miriam. "We can't be! We will find them." But in her heart of hearts she was beginning to think the same as Sam, that something awful must have happened to their friends. They'd surely have been in touch by now.

"Pssst!"

"What?" said Sam.

"It wasn't me," said Miriam turning back to where the noise had come from.

"Probably another one of those stupid Rasperites following us," said Sam. "Take no notice." He began to walk up the Avenue. "I am so sick of...."

"Pssst!"

They both turned.

There was no-one there.

"Whoever you are, go away!" Sam had had enough.

"It's me, Belle Fellows!"

They peered into the darkness.

"Over here. I'm in the bushes. Make sure no-one is following you."

Sam looked around. There was nothing but the dark Avenue and the laughter of the Rasperites from behind the wall.

"Come on! Now!" Belle hissed.

They went quickly towards the sound of her voice. Miriam suddenly yelped. Something had grabbed her ankle. "Be quiet, will you? It's me!" Belle pulled them both into the bushes. "I've been trying to talk to you for ages, but everywhere you went, you had a stupid Rasperite behind you!"

"It's not our fault," said Miriam. "We couldn't get rid of them."

"It's the same for me," whispered Belle. "I've been followed everywhere by that horrible fat Flouncy Willis. That's why I haven't told you."

"Told us what?" asked Sam. He could hardly see Belle for the gloom.

"I know where the others are."

"You know where Alice is...!"

"Ssssh," whispered Belle. "I've been taking them food."

"They're safe!" Sam couldn't help shouting it out.

"If you don't be quiet we'll have Willis flopping around. It's already taken me two hours to lose him. They want me to bring you to them."

"Who?"

"The three of them, Sam, why aren't you listening?"

"When?"

"Be on the Green at midnight. Willis will probably be too drunk to follow me by then anyway."

"Where are they?" whispered Miriam

"You'll find out."

"How did they get out of the Town Hall"

"You'll find that out too. Go now. And don't look back."

"Alright," said Sam. "See you at mid..."

"And another thing," said Belle grabbing his arm. "We're all getting old! That's what's happening to us. I noticed it first when my cut wouldn't heal and your voice started to go funny, and Mr Pen started getting backache, and everyone was getting hungry, and lots of other things. You're not twelve and always will be anymore. You're growing up. Oh and bring lots of things to eat. And candles." And with that Belle was gone. She'd disappeared into the darkness of the bushes.

"Getting old?" said Miriam with her eyebrows arched, "What's that?"

A DANGEROUS JOURNEY

Sam and Miriam left his house as it began to get dark. They carried a big bag of food, candles and warm clothing. Sam had reasoned that wherever the others were if they needed candles they probably didn't have any heat. They waited in the shadows of the trees on the Green.

The first words they heard were, "Hurry up. I think I'm being followed."

"Who by?" asked Sam as Belle appeared out of the gloom.

"I told you, Willis. He must have left the People's cafe early. Come on."

They crept behind Belle across the Green, flitting from the shadow of one tree to another, then ducked down alleys and crept up Lanes, crossed Circles and avoided Avenues. If anyone was following them, and especially if it was the fat and wheezing Flouncy Willis, they would certainly have been lost within ten minutes. Finally Belle led them along by a huge fence and they sat down crammed in between two dustbins. She pulled an old tarpaulin over them.

"We'll be safe here," she said. "Then we'll have to wait till the Rasperites have finished working in the mine."

"The mine?" said Sam in surprise.

"They're in the goldmine. Don't you know where you are? This is the fence round it."

Belle's twisting and turning route had even fooled Sam. He looked up at the fence and recognised it at once. "I thought the goldmine was closed."

"It was," said Belle, "but they've opened parts of it again now to get gold for the walls of the Great Hall."

"How did the three of them get down there?"

"They escaped out of the basement in the Town Hall. The Rasperites left them there without any food."

"No food!"

"Alice thinks they would have starved if I hadn't found them and let them out."

"Starved?"

"Yes, starved to nothing." replied Belle with huge round eyes as if she couldn't believe it either.

"How did you let them out?" asked Sam. "I was outside and watched all night."

"I know," she whispered, "I saw you, but I couldn't talk to you cos there were too many Rasperites around. I knew a tiny window in the bottom of the wall that had been boarded up. Except it wasn't boarded up now, because I fell through it a couple of months ago. I got in there again as soon as I had a chance after I'd seen them all being arrested. And as soon as the Rasperites had gone it was easy to get down to the basement and unbolt the door."

"Well done, Belle, that's brilliant," said Sam, in genuine admiration. "But how did you get them away from the Town Hall?"

"The window is so low we must have been in the shadows," she said. "That's why you didn't see us. Then we crossed the town in the dark. It was Alice's idea to go down the mine, and we were lucky we got there before they opened it up again. Since then I've been taking them food and candles."

Sam's admiration for Belle was rising in leaps and bounds.

"Anyway its time for us to go," she said getting up and leading them along by the fence. "Through here," she whispered and she pushed them through a small hole and into the huge yard of the mine. It was very dark and the drilling machinery cast long and frightening shadows.

"Wait," whispered Belle, pulling them back into the shadows. "There's some Rasperites still here."

They crouched in the darkness as the last of the miners left and then quickly crossed the yard to a huge wooden tower.

"This is the lift," she said, "and it's the worst part."

They climbed into the lift and Belle pulled a lever. Suddenly the night was filled with a terrible clanking sound and the enormous wheel at the top of the tower began to turn.

"Someone will notice!" Sam had to shout to make himself heard.

"They'll think it's the wind," said Belle. "I usually climb down, but it would be too difficult to show both of you how."

She smiled at Sam, and it was only then that he realised the risk she was taking for them. They could easily have been caught. It was like Rasper was making everybody he knew as brave as they could possibly be. They stepped into the lift and it plunged down into the darkness of the mine, making their stomachs lurch.

"I'm going to be sick," said Miriam.

"Hold on," said Belle.

Suddenly they stopped with a jolt at the bottom of the shaft. They couldn't see a thing. Belle lit a small lamp she'd taken from her bag and they stumbled off uncertainly into the shadows of a huge tunnel. There were tracks on the floor for the iron carts that were used to haul the rock and ore, and they could just make out the tools of the miners stacked against the walls. They moved quickly down the tunnel. Suddenly from behind them they heard the terrible cranking of the lift again.

Belle turned back, "Someone did hear," she said.

There were voices behind them in the direction of the lift.

"I can hear them," said Sam. "They're behind us."

"Quick jump in this," said Belle, "The track goes downhill from here."

She pulled a mining cart out from a side junction and Sam and Miriam climbed in as quickly as they could. Belle gave it a push and soon it began to rumble along the tracks taking them down into the mine. After a while the voices began to fade, but somehow that only made it even more scary. It was pitch-black and silent except for the rumbling of the cart's wheels as they rushed headlong down and down through the dark.

"Nearly there," said Belle. And suddenly she pulled up on the brake. Sam almost fell out as the cart came to a dead stop.

"Oops sorry!" said Belle.

"It's alright," said Sam rubbing his side. "Just give me a warning next time."

"I said, we were nearly there."

"But you didn't say we were going to stop immediately, did you?"

"Well if you don't like the cart, you can try your knees," she said, as she shone her lamp into a small side tunnel which couldn't have been more than two feet high. "You can go first, Sam. Seeing as you want to criticise me all the time."

"I wasn't criticising," said Sam, "I was just saying..." He didn't bother to argue but got down and started to crawl into the tiny tunnel. What followed was probably the worst half hour of their lives. Water dripped onto their backs and sharp rocks cut their knees. Their hands clutched the mud, their backs brushed the tunnel top and their skin was rubbed raw. Sam was in agony as he dragged the heavy bag of food behind him, but he wasn't going to admit it to Belle. He just kept going.

"How much longer is it?" moaned Miriam, who was behind Belle.

"Not much further," she said. "Look, you can see the tunnel is getting higher."

Sam looked. It seemed as if the tunnel was opening up.

Finally Belle said, "You can stand up now."

Sam and Miriam got unsteadily to their feet. As they rubbed their knees they could see that they were in what seemed to be a large underground cavern with a small river of black water leading to a dark lake in the middle. There was what looked like an old boat pulled up on the mud.

"Up here," Belle clambered up a pile of rocks. They followed and after a few seconds they could see a dark opening ahead of them.

"Come on," said Belle.

They carried on up until they could see a light flickering.

"Here we are," said Belle.

And suddenly they were inside a large cave. There was a small fire burning and around it sat Alice, Fortuna and Jack.

"Sam!" Alice jumped up and hugged him. And so did Fortuna. She looked tired and dirty, but smiled at Sam all the same. Jack as usual was jumping with excitement.

"How long...?"

"Is that where you sleep?"

"What do you do with the boat?"

Sam and Miriam were full of questions.

"Wait," said Alice. "Have something to eat first, then sleep, and afterwards we'll talk."

Sam was too tired to argue, and he could see that Miriam's eyes were beginning to droop in the heat from the fire. They lay on some old blankets and within minutes they were asleep.

DOWN THE GOLDMINE

It was dark when they woke up and they had no idea what time it was. Alice said that you could tell it was morning by the sound of the men working in the new shafts. Jack was putting timber from the old mine workings onto the fire and Sam noticed for the first time that the cave they were in was high and narrow.

"I think it's a shaft they must have started once but didn't finish," said Alice. "They probably didn't find any gold here, that's why they don't come any more." Her voice echoed a little around the rocks.

"But they might come back," said Miriam looking worried.

"They must know we're here," said Sam slowly. "We used the lift. We thought they were following us down."

"They might have thought it was other miners stealing gold." said Alice.

"Stealing?" said Sam. "Are people stealing now in Thistown?"

"Don't worry, they're so stupid, they probably won't even check," said Alice with a smile.

Sam was pleased to see that Alice seemed to have all her old spirit back, even in these uncomfortable surroundings.

"We won't be able to use it again to get out though, will we?" said Fortuna. "They're bound to check if they see it used in the middle of the night *twice*." She seemed even angrier than usual.

"How will we get out then?" asked Miriam looking round at the cold, wet rock. "You are not thinking of staying here forever, are you?"

"Someone's missing," said Alice. "Didn't you notice?"

Sam looked round, "Belle? Where's Belle?"

"She went back up hours ago to get us more supplies. If she can go up and down then so can we!" She'll show us," said Alice. "Simple!"

"Oh," sighed Miriam, remembering the way down and hoping the way up might be a little easier.

"Why did you want us to come down away?" said Sam slowly. He was watching Alice and knew there was something on her mind.

"To say hullo!" said Alice brightly.

"Hello," said Sam. And he smiled his slow smile back at her.

"We need your help," said Fortuna getting down to business.

"We've decided to get rid of Rasper, you see?" said Alice.

"Just like that?" said Miriam, horrified at the thought.

"We'll throw him in the cornfields if we have to." said Fortuna. Sam was shocked to hear her talk like that. He was beginning to think that there was sometimes something *too* angry about Fortuna.

"Yeah! Rasper's got to go!" Jack jumped up. "He's ruining everything!"

"But how do we get rid of him?" Sam asked. Like Miriam, he couldn't imagine how they could do it. "Rasper controls everything. He's building a Great Hall. Vincente's doing a huge painting of the No-Life Man. No-one can move without one of Rasper's spies running to the police or one of the Rasperites. Everyone's scared of him."

"Belle's told us all about it," said Fortuna.

"So how will you do it then?" asked Miriam again.

"We don't know," said Alice. "We were hoping that you might be able to think of something."

"You thought I might know?" Sam looked round at their hopeful, waiting faces.

"You always used to think of things," said Alice. "Didn't you once have a design for a new Town Hall?"

"Which you trod on!" said Sam. "I don't know how to get rid of Rasper any more than you do! I've been racking my brains for days trying to work out what to do, but I don't know either. I'm very sorry. I wish I did."

He looked sad, as if he was letting them all down, but what else could he say? They were sitting hundreds of feet below the ground while Rasper rampaged above them, and the Rasperites lead by Henry Horne and Bill Rory terrified everyone. What Rasper was doing was just too big for them. Sam told them about the Rasperites smashing up the Opinion's printing presses and it all seemed worse. They sat staring as the flames licked round the wood on the fire. What could they do? No-one said anything. They were too depressed.

A few hours later Belle came back down. She brought food and an extraordinary bit of news.

"There's another No-Life Man," she said.

They stared at her in shock.

"A donkey cart ran over one of the carpenters working on the Great Hall. He didn't get up so they took him down to the Hospital, but Stitch and Slice couldn't heal him, and he stopped breathing. They said the life had gone out of him."

"Carts have run over people before," said Sam, "but the life hasn't gone out of them."

"It did this time," said Belle. "He's called Tom Chipper and lives on the Tenth Circle. Or he used to. Now he's in the cornfields."

"They threw him in?" asked Fortuna. "Into the corn?"

"Yes," said Belle, "And..." she waited a second and then added, "he didn't disappear."

"He didn't disappear?" said Alice. "Why not?"

Belle shrugged. "No-one knows. He stopped breathing at the hospital, they threw him in and now he's like the other No-Life Man. He just lies there in the corn and his skin's started going brown already."

They all stared at Belle.

"Two No-Life Men?" Alice looked at Sam.

He remembered Peter the Pipe and Walton Wall who'd fallen off the Old Tower into the corn. They'd disappeared immediately. So what was the difference between them, and the first No-Life Man who wouldn't disappear, and now this carpenter, Tom Chipper, who wouldn't disappear either?

"Rasper used the No-Life Man to become leader of the Assembly," said Fortuna angrily, "And now there's another No-Life Man for him to use!"

"What we have to do," said Sam, "is think about it, and find out how it all started."

"We know how it started." said Fortuna. "With the first No-Life Man!"

"Yes," said Sam. "But we have to find out where he came from."

"What good will that do us?" asked Jack.

"Because if we know how things start, we might find out how they end," said Sam.

"And how are we going to find out how things started?" Fortuna was getting even more angry. "What we have to do is get rid of Rasper! That's it!"

"Yes!" shouted Jack, "Get rid of him. In any way at all! Make him into a No-Life Man!"

"No," said Sam, "First..." but no-one was listening to him.

"And how are we going to do make Rasper a No-Life Man?" Alice asked Jack. "Just as a matter of interest?"

"How should I know?"

"We'll find out. And if you all don't, I will." said Fortuna quietly. "Believe me, I'll find out how to get rid of him."

No-one said anything. Fortuna could be very frightening sometimes.

"Well you can't stay down here forever," said Belle unhappily. "Sorry, but I'm going to get caught bringing this food down one of these days, and then what will happen? You'll starve down here instead of in the Town Hall basement."

This thought silenced them. They seemed to be right back at the beginning.

Finally Alice said, "Belle's right, we can't stay down here, but at least we have somewhere to go now."

"Where?" asked Fortuna looking up.

"Sam told us, didn't he? He said that Rasper had smashed up Mr Pen's printing works. We'll go there. The Rasperites have already been in there, so why should they go back?"

"And then what we will do?" said Miriam.

"We'll think of something," said Alice brightly.

"It's better than sitting here arguing anyway," said Belle.

"How will we get up?" asked Miriam, dreading the journey back.

"We'll go up in the lift," said Alice. "It'll be the last time, so it won't matter if somebody does see it."

"They won't see it." said Belle. "Rasper's having another meeting. Everybody has to go, so the whole town will be on the Green."

"When is it?" asked Sam.

"Tonight," said Belle with a grin, "So I think we'd better get ready."

COMING UP TO RASPER

They left the remainder of their food and candles in the cave in case they ever had to come back and hide again. As soon as they heard the men in the mine stop their work, they crept back past the underground lake and the old boat, and made their way to the low tunnel. Miriam and Sam still both had sore knees from the last time, but they crawled over the hard rock with the water dripping on their backs again without complaining. This time they couldn't use the cart because they were going up hill and not down, so they walked back up to the lift shaft. Belle clambered up ahead to see if the coast was clear. It seemed to be, so they started the lift and got in. The noise it made as it clanked its way to the surface seemed loud enough to alert the whole town and they were sure that by the time they came to the top, everyone would be there to welcome them.

But there was no-one. They were all on the Green. As they walked down Avenue R they heard Rasper's amplified voice echoing over the rooftops.

"We've nearly finished the Great Hall," he was saying. "Our great artist, Vincente Smith will soon put the painting of the No-Life Man onto the wall facing the Cornfields. And he will show us the way to cross them!"

"Oh please, I don't want to listen to any more of this," said Miriam as they crossed the Twenty-Third Circle.

"I'd like to starve him!" said Jack.

"Like he would have done to us," spat Fortuna.

"Anyway," said Sam, "the first problem is to get to the Opinion building."

By the time they reached the Second Circle they could see the Green was packed. Everybody in the town was there. They crept around the shadows of The Green. Every now and again they could see through the backs of the crowd to Rasper on the Town Hall balcony. Hundreds of lights burned behind him, and the usual huge blue banners fluttered down beneath him. His voice was already hoarse as he shouted through the microphone. "More work! More effort! And soon we shall have the great opening ceremony of the Great.....!"

Jack slammed the back door of the Opinion building as they went in and Rasper's voice was cut off. They went quietly up the stairs and into the old print room. They stood silently as they looked around the smashed printing presses. It wasn't very welcoming.

Belle said quickly, "I can get you blankets and a cooking stove, and a lamp to read by."

No-one spoke. The broken machinery, the cold floor and the sound of the Rasper's voice once again through the broken windows was enough to make anyone depressed. His voice boomed, "And I, the Great Listener to the No-Life Man shall lead you...."

"The Great Listener? Is that what he calls himself now?" asked Miriam.

"And sometimes, the Great Ear," said Belle.

THE UNDERGROUND

After what seemed an age the crowd below began to go home. Sam sat down with his back to the wall on one of the blankets that Belle had brought. Alice quietly sat opposite him as he unfurled a ball of paper he'd found on the floor. It was the letter that Miriam had written, and Rasper had screwed up. Sam showed it to Alice.

"Oh Miri! " she said, "Everyone should read it. There must be others like us out there. They can't all want Rasper."

"They don't. But they don't know what to do, that's all," said Belle. "Like us."

"Then we'll have to show them, won't we?" said Alice.

"We tried that, Alice," said Sam staring at the broken presses. And look what happened?"

"Well, we'll have to try again."

"You're going to mend all these, are you?" asked Sam.

"There must be some other way," said Alice.

"Posters!" said Fortuna suddenly.

"Posters? What posters?" asked Jack.

"Our posters! Saying what we want. About Rasper!" Fortuna said excitedly.

"He'll just tear them down," said Miriam.

"Not if there are hundreds of them!"

"How are we going to make hundreds of posters?" Sam wanted to know.

"Alice said it. Others like us. They'll help us. It's obvious. They won't all be Rasperites, will they?" said Fortuna.

"How will we know if they are, or if they aren't?" asked Miriam.

"We'll have to be clever and find out who's side they're on." said Fortuna.

"It's very dangerous," said Miriam "We make one mistake and we'll be handed over to Rasper."

"What else do we do? Sit here until we go rotten like the No-Life Men?" asked Fortuna. "Well you can. I'm not."

"We have to try something," said Alice.

"We have to get other people!" Fortuna almost shouted it. "Then we'll all make posters and we'll stick them up - at night. And even if the Rasperites do rip them down, at least they'll have been up for a few hours and people will have seen them and then they'll know that there are others who hate Rasper like they do! It's brilliant!"

"Well as it was my idea in the first place, I agree," said Alice.

"So who do we get then?" asked Fortuna looking round almost as if she was daring anyone to disagree with her.

"There's Tess the Dress on the Seventh Circle," said Miriam. "I know she'd be with us."

"And Mary on Avenue T!" said Fortuna,

"Ray from Avenue X." This was Jack.

As they all thought of their old friends they began to feel more optimistic.

"Jonny Ridgewood and Glen Green," said Alice.

"You mean the Green Runner?" asked Miriam.

"Yes!" said Alice I know he'd want to be here. It'll save him spending his days running round the circles!"

"And Baz Brick! He'll be with us" said Fortuna excitedly. "We'll make a list and divide them up between us, "

"There'll be at least a dozen," said Jack.

"When shall we ask them to come?" said Sam.

"The sooner the better," said Alice.

"Tomorrow night. They can all come here," said Fortuna.

"It will be very dangerous," said Sam, "You'll have to watch what you say. Because if you get it wrong and the person you are talking to is really a Rasperite, then he'll find out about the meeting and come himself with Henry Horne and Bill Rory."

"Yes, of course, Sam." Alice mocked him.

"You weren't here when they did this!" Sam said angrily as he pointed at the smashed machinery. "They had hammers and iron bars."

"Sorry, Sam," said Alice.

"You don't understand," he said, "Miri and me spent a long time looking for you. We went round all the circles. One night we saw the Rasperites pulling a donkey into a big shed. I think they took the life from him."

"They did," said Belle sadly. "They do it all the time to make a big carpet of donkey skins for the Great Hall."

"Taking a donkey's life to make a carpet?" Miriam couldn't believe it. She remembered the donkey shrieking as it was pulled through the doorway.

"They cut the donkey's throat with a knife," said Belle. Miriam gasped.

"That's why we have to get rid of them," said Alice.

"We're really going to start something!" said Fortuna. She stood up. "Finally something against Rasper! It's like a new thing! A new thing for everybody. But what do we call it? We have to give it a name. What do we call it?"

Belle said, "The goldmine! That's where it started."

"No," said Fortuna, "Because then they'll know where we were."

"The Underground!" said Alice. "We'll call it The Underground. Because we are never seen, but we are always there. Like under the ground."

"The Underground?" Fortuna wasn't so sure.

"Yeah!" Jack was. "The Underground! I like it!"

"How are we going to do posters anyway?" asked Miriam, "We haven't got any paper."

"Yes we have. Here!" Belle pulled a huge roll she'd seen from under a broken printing press. The Rasperites didn't get this."

"All we need now is brushes and paint," said Alice.

"There are some here!" said Belle scrabbling around the floor. She looked at the tiny handful of pens and pencils she'd picked up, "But nowhere near enough. Not if there's a dozen of us making posters. "

There was a silence then Alice said, "Vincente Smith! Didn't Rasper say that he was painting a huge portrait of the No-Life Man for the Great Hall? He'll have paints, won't he? We'll get them from him."

"How will you get them?" asked Miriam, looking very worried.

"I'll ask him." said Alice simply. "I'm sure he'll help us. Didn't you help him make an easel once, Sam?"

Sam nodded.

"And I think it's so good that we'll use paint meant for the Great hall to make posters that say, 'Down with Rasper!" Alice was delighted by her own idea.

"Yes, but..." Sam didn't want to say how dangerous it would be for her to go and find Vincente.

Miriam said it for him, "You can't go, Alice. Vincente's working in the Great Hall. He's surrounded by Rasperites! They will catch you!"

"Not if I go in disguise," smiled Alice. "Don't all Rasperites wear blue uniforms now? Why don't I wear a blue uniform too?"

"I know where I can get you one." said Belle, "Just ask me. I know where to get everything."

"I'll go," said Sam. "I don't need a uniform.

"It was my idea!" said Alice. "Anyway I want to see this new Great Hall."

"Well this time, Alice," said Sam firmly, "I'm coming with you. I'm followed by Rasperites everywhere anyway. So you can follow me instead."

"Oh very sensible, Sam," smiled Alice, but she was pleased he was going to be with her.

"And the rest of us," said Fortuna, "will go and find our friends."

Jack raised his fist in the air. "For the Underground!"

Fortuna raised her fist too. "The Underground!"

THE GREAT PAINTER

It had taken Belle no time at all to find a uniform for Alice. She'd seen them stored in great piles in a room at the back of the Town Hall, and had gone straight there and got in through her little window. But once inside she'd heard several of the Browncoat Boys coming and so had to hide in the piles of uniforms. It wasn't until nearly morning that she was able to came back with a bright blue Rasperite jacket and trousers.

"I hope they fit," Belle said, "I didn't want to turn the light on, so I had to feel for the right size."

Quite miraculously they seemed as though they'd been made for Alice and she paraded around the broken presses as if she'd become a fully fledged Rasperite.

"I am the great listener. I am the great ear-hole!" she laughed delightedly. Then she tucked her hair up into a Rasperite hat and borrowed a pair of glasses from Sam.

"You look just like Alice Bright," said Sam pessimistically.

"You'd say that whatever I was wearing," said Alice. "Shall we go?"

The others wished them luck. Miriam seemed especially worried, "Alice...."

"Don't worry, Miri, nothing will ever happen to me!" said Alice as she kissed her goodbye.

Sam was already by the door and they crept down the stairs The sun was just coming up as they came quickly out of the back of the Opinion building.

"Go on then," whispered Alice. "You cross the Green and I'll look as if I'm following you."

"Rasperites don't slouch about, so keep your back straight." he whispered back sternly.

"Don't worry about me. Just go."

Sam walked off across the Green pretending a confidence he didn't feel as Rasperite Alice followed, flitting from tree to tree. Finally they were across the Green and began the long walk up Avenue A to the Great Hall.

Since the appearance of the second No-Life Man, no-one would use the great donkey carts anymore in case they were run over, so now hundreds of men and women were hauling huge loads of rock and stone on their backs up towards the Hall. It was a sorry sight. As Sam and the Alice walked past them and looked at their chalk-smeared, unhappy faces and at the Rasperites in their blue uniforms goading them on, they thought their new Underground movement might get more people joining it than they'd thought.

The entrance to the Great Hall was already finished. It was a huge arch and to their horror they saw that at the centre of it was a carved figure of Rasper covered in gold. Down either side of the arch were images of the people of Thistown kneeling at his feet and looking up at him as though they were worshipping their hero.

"Look at that!" whispered Alice. "It's as if they think he's some kind of saviour!" She was feeling more confident now and decided to join Sam as the workmen bustled around them. They looked up at the arch. Around the top was written in huge letters, *The Great Hall of the No-Life Man,* and around the inside, beneath Rasper's golden feet, *Rasper, the Great Listener, Leads his People.* It was so huge, and so grand, and already seeming so permanent that even Alice had a moment of doubt. Could they ever beat Rasper?

Sam whispered, "I'll find Vincente." They'd decided it was better that Sam spoke to the painter because he'd worked with him before. "You stay here and keep a look out."

He went quickly as above them a huge wooden beam suspended by ropes held by what seemed like dozens of straining workers was slotted into place in the roof. The noise and dust was incredible.

A Rasperite was shouting at a group of workmen, "You there! Get on with it! Do you think the No-Life Man can wait for you! Hurry up, or Rasper will see to you!"

The workmen pushed at their barrows and shovelled their sand. Sweat poured down from their foreheads. Alice had never seen people work harder. There were hundreds of them crawling over the vast structure of the Great Hall like thousands of ants.

Her thoughts were suddenly interrupted by a voice hissing in her ear, "Don't I know you?"

She turned quickly to see Lester Lean, a cross-eyed man who used to be a gardener on the Green.

"I don't think so," she said, although she knew exactly who he was.

Lester leaned in and looked at her closely, "Yes I do, you're..."

"Arliss Broom ," said Alice with a perfectly straight face. It was the first thing that had come into her head and she had no idea where it came from.

"Arliss Broom?" Lester sniggered.

"Do you think it's funny," said Alice with a hard face. "Are you insulting the uniform of a Rasperite?"

"Oh no," said Lester, "Oh no. Sorry, I thought you was someone else" And he looked carefully at Alice again.

"I'm an Inspector in the Great Rasper Construction Effort," said Alice as she watched three men tipping a huge bucket of sand onto the floor. "If that sand isn't perfect then they they won't make proper concrete and the walls will crumble, won't they? Nothing to snigger about is it?"

"Ah. Sorry." said Lester, terrified now in case he should upset an important Rasperite.

"Who are you anyway?" asked Alice.

"I'm Undermaster Lean in the Great March of Rasperdom," he said and proudly smoothed his blue overalls.

"And have you any idea of what the Great March of Rasperdom is?" asked Alice in a superior way as if she was testing him, but actually wanting to know what it was herself.

"It's us." Lester said proudly and waved his arms at all the blue suits working around them. "We are the Great March. It's an organisation!"

"For what?" Alice asked sternly.

"Ah, for Rasper."

"It's obviously for Rasper," said Alice. "Try and be a bit more precise. After all you owe him everything, don't you?"

"Oh yes."

"So what is it?"

"Ah?" Lester was getting worried now. He didn't want to look as though he didn't know what the Great March of Rasperdom was, especially in front of an official. "I'm sorry if I've offended you," he said.

"I think I'll report you," said Alice, "For not knowing the great works of Rasper."

"Oh no, please don't do that. Please." Lester was grovelling by now. "I know it's all to improve our ear."

"Our ear? Yes go on. Let's see if you know a bit more than that." Alice was getting interested by now.

"Our *inner ear*, Madam."

"Go on, don't keep stopping, or I'll report you for *hesitation!*"

"Oh, I didn't mean to *hesitate*," said Lester speeding up, "You see, the inner ear is our *special ear*, which is the ear we use to listen to the voice of the No-Life Man from over the cornfields." He stopped, obviously very pleased with himself for having remembered it. Then he added, "And if we do what Rasper tells us, we can hear the voice even better. Not as good as Rasper, of course, because he is the *Great Ear*. But we can try. You do it like this." He stood very still with one ear cocked towards the cornfields.

Alice had no idea what he expected to hear, apart from the shriek of the wind. "Very good, Undermaster Lean, very good." she said, "And what else?"

"What else," asked Lester getting panicky.

"Yes, all of it. I want to see how much you know of the Great Works of Rasper."

And she made Lester recite every piece of Rasper nonsense he knew, over and over again.

Meanwhile Sam had walked further into the hall. It was so magnificent it nearly took his breath away. There were huge carved panels all around the walls and ahead of him the biggest window he'd ever seen looking out over the cornfields.

He felt a nudge in his back. "Out! Out! Out of my way!"

Sam turned to see the huge beard and glaring, mad eyes of Vincente Smith, Thistown's famous painter. "Can't you see I'm wowowoworking," he stammered.

"I'm sorry, Vincente," said Sam, "Don't you remember me?"

Vincente stared, then he stuttered, "S-S-S-Sam! Is it you?"

"Yes, but don't say it too loud."

"Why not?"

"Because...." Sam was going to explain, then he realised that Vincente was too wrapped up in his painting to have any idea of anything that had happened to him, or anything else at all, come to that.

"You're m-my easel man!" Vincente suddenly exclaimed. "It's my favourite easel. I still use it, you know? I wish I was back in my studio, using it now. "

"Why, Vincente? What's wrong?" asked Sam.

"Look," he said. "And pointed up towards the vast Wall of the Great Hall towering above them. On it was a huge drawing of the No-Life Man. It hadn't been painted yet, just sketched in.

"What do you think?" Vincente asked sadly.

"Ah...?" Sam wasn't sure what to say.

"It's alright, Sam, you can be honest with me. It's terrible isn't it? I didn't want to do it, you see?" He looked at Sam with great wet eyes, "I didn't want to do it at all."

"It's not so bad," Sam said, trying to console him.

"You can't fool me. If there's one thing I never wanted to paint, it's that!"

Sam didn't know what to say. Vincente looked as if he was about to cry. Sam hardly had the heart to ask him if he had any paint to spare. Vincente looked like a sorry, unhappy child. Sam touched him gently on the shoulder and as Vincente looked up with a sorry smile Sam suddenly understood. He froze as he remembered the Hospital and their first sighting of the No-Life Man. He remembered that the No-Life Man had reminded him of someone. And now he knew who that someone was. It was Vincente!

"Vincente," he said gently. "Can you tell me something?"

It was a long time later that he walked back under the arch with a huge bag of paints. He found Alice and they walked up Avenue A together. His head was buzzing with what he'd heard from Vincente and he was relieved when Alice said she going to recruit a new member of the Underground. He needed time to think.

JONNY RIDGEWOOD

Jonny got his name from living on the only ridge in Thistown. It ran across the Great Park between the Fifteenth and Thirty-fifth Circle between Avenues M and K. There weren't many houses up there and it was quite easy for Alice to go quietly through the trees, hide her Rasperite uniform under a bush, and creep forward in the dark up to Jonny's front door.

She was quite nervous. Although she had known Jonny a long time she wasn't sure how you could really tell if someone was telling the truth when they said they were against Rasper? Or come to that, if they said the opposite? Lies were unknown in Thistown before Rasper, but now they were everywhere. And how would she know what to think about Jonny?

Jonny, like Alice, was twelve, would have always been twelve etc - but that was before everyone had started growing older as Belle had found out. Perhaps soon they'd all be fourteen, and then...? Alice could hardly tell about herself, let alone Jonny. All she knew was that the short and fiery black boy had always been her friend, and she hoped that he still would be.

She came quickly out of the shadows and tapped quietly on the door. There was no reply. She tapped again and the door swung open. What did that mean? Hardly anyone used to lock their doors in Thistown, but now they nearly all did. Did it mean that Jonny still clung to the old ways and could still be trusted, or did it mean that something had happened to him, or did it mean that...." There were so many possibilities that Alice could think of. It was very difficult this business of learning how to trust people all over again.

She decided that as she'd come this far, she may as well go on. She pushed the door further open and went into the short dark hallway. The first thing she saw was a cat, and then a blue Rasperite jacket! What did that mean? That Jonny had joined the Rasperites? That he was having a meal with some of them perhaps? The thought of finding Jonny sitting at a table with Henry Horne and Bill Rory quite terrified her. She certainly didn't want to end the evening back in the Town Hall basement. She was sure that Belle wouldn't find it so easy to get them out again. She decided that all things considered it was better that she leave and go back to the relative safety of the print works, and had actually turned to run out, when the door to the living room opened. Alice froze, but to her delight she saw that it was only another cat coming out.

She squeezed herself against the hall wall to peer into the living room and all she could see was the red glow of a fire and a pair of feet. Did they belong to Jonny, or to some other Rasperite who'd taken his or her shoes off? Alice couldn't make up her mind. They were quite small feet, so they might have been Jonny's, but on the other hand they wore thick grey socks and she was sure Jonny didn't wear those. Once again she decided that the house was full of Rasperites and was about to go when she heard, "Who's there?"

The voice was unmistakably Jonny's. But was he there on his own? Alice was still trying to make up her mind when the door opened and there stood Jonny in a blue shirt, blue Rasper slacks and grey socks.

"Hello, Alice," he said, smiling in a very friendly way.

"I'm sorry," Alice quaked, "I seem to have come to the wrong place."

"Come in." Jonny smiled, "What do you mean the wrong place?"

Alice thought for a minute of saying that she'd knocked on the wrong door, but that would have been ridiculous. She'd known Jonny for as long as she could remember, and been to the house hundreds of times, and anyway there weren't any other houses nearby on the ridge. He was standing there watching her carefully, his eyes huge in his black and serious face. Alice didn't know what to say. This was the same old Jonny, a bit small, but very strong, standing there looking as intense as he usually did. After a long pause she finally just said, "Jonny?"

Jonny smiled again, "That's me." And he opened the door fully to reveal a welcoming fire and an empty room.

"I thought you might have someone else with you," said Alice.

"Oh yes, Rasper's in the kitchen."

"What?"

Jonny laughed, "Can't you take a joke? Why would I want him in my kitchen?"

"I don't know, I..." Alice still wasn't sure.

"Why don't you come in? You'll get cold out there."

One of the cats was rubbing against her leg. Alice took this as a good sign. and went in and immediately asked, "There's no-one upstairs is there?

"No," said Jonny smiling, "And no-one in the garden either. Did you recover from being down the mine?"

"How did you know about that?" Alice asked in shock.

"Oh I hear about things," Jonny said. "I'm sorry. I've worried you. Let me get you something to drink." And he went towards the kitchen.

"Long live Rasper!" said Alice as she watched the blue uniform disappear through the door.

Jonny turned back, "You don't mean that do you?"

Alice didn't know what to say. It seemed that she was the one being tested now. "I.. er....I don't know," she mumbled foolishly.

Jonny went over and kissed her cheek. "You're not a very good spy, are you?"

"Aren't I?" said Alice.

"I saw you on the front page of the Clarion." said Jonny.

"Oh that was a mistake. I like Rasper really!"

Jonny slammed the kitchen door nearly catching a cat's tail in it. "Well if you want to know, I hate him. And what I hate about him most is that he's made all of us suspicious of each other. And that's just too bad, because we all used to be friends."

Alice still wasn't quite sure but she decided honesty was the best policy and took her courage in both hands and said, "I hate Rasper too and I think he's the worst thing ever to have happened to Thistown. So now you can tie me up if you want and take me down to Awkward Corner and starve me! I don't care! I hate Rasper!"

"I'll make you that drink," said Jonny, opening the door again. " I think you need one."

"Are you really not a Rasperite?"

"Of course not."

"Why are you wearing a Rasperite uniform?"

"Because like everyone else, I'm pretending."

"Is everyone pretending?" asked Alice.

"Well who would really like Rasper?" said Jonny. "Except a few fools from Awkward Corner? And who, in their right minds, would wear socks like these?"

That made Alice's mind up. Only the old Jonny would complain about the socks.

"And I'll tell you something else," Jonny went on, " I'd cut this horrible uniform up into a thousand pieces and burn it if I could!"

"Oh, thank goodness for that." Alice sank down into a chair.

"Has it been very bad?" Jonny asked.

"Very," said Alice, and felt like she'd like to burst into tears.

"Don't worry," Jonny knelt beside her, "I'll help in any way I can."

Alice was sorry she'd ever doubted him. She immediately told him about the Underground and the meeting they were having later that night. They talked for a long time until finally Alice went, leaving Jonny standing at his door, stroking his favourite cat and promising he'd come. As Alice walked back through the trees, she felt a

great anger at Rasper. How many other people were having to wear those horrible uniforms and lie to everyone
because of him?

THE BEGINNING

By the time Alice got back to the Workshop, the others were already there. As Sam mixed the paints for the posters, they told Alice how they'd spread out in the darkness of the town to find their other friends. Several times they'd nearly been caught. Jack Juniper told how he had dodged the Rasperites to find Avenue X, Ray; Fortuna was convinced that Tessa (or Tess the Dress as she was usually called because of her wild clothes) would be joining them, but had only managed to leave a message for Avenue T Mary. Only Belle had been unsuccessful, but as she'd done so much already, no-one had expected too much of her. They were all very satisfied with themselves except Miriam who had looked very sad ever since she'd arrived.

"What's the matter, Miri?" asked Sam.

"There's more," she said.

"More what?"

"More No-life Men and now even a No-Life Woman."

They were shocked.

"Who?" Alice asked.

"When I was hiding by the People's cafe I heard two Rasperites coming back from a party." said Miriam. "They were talking about a big wooden beam that fell down from the roof of the Great Hall onto two people, knocking the life out of them. One was a stonemason called Richard Etchard and the other one was a Rasperite called Lester Lean."

"Lester!" Alice exclaimed. "I was talking to him today!" She immediately began to feel guilty at making him recite Rasper's philosophies over and over again. "Are you saying, he's got no life now?"

"None at all" said Miriam quietly. "They decided not to throw them into the corn because they knew they wouldn't disappear, so they just put them under a big pile of old stones."

"You said there was a woman too." said Sam.

"She was nothing to do with the Great Hall," tears were welling up in Miriam's doleful grey eyes, "I knew her. We all did. It was Martha."

Old Martha. Everyone knew her. She was the oldest person in Thistown. She was a hundred and five years old, had always been a hundred and five etc Except now she wasn't.

"Perhaps the life will come back to her," said Sam sadly.

"It never has before to anyone else," said Alice.

"How did it happen to Martha?" asked Sam.

"No-one knows," said Miriam. "She went to bed and the life went out of her. There didn't seem to be a reason."

"Perhaps the Life will go out of us all sometime," said Alice sadly.

"How ?" said Jack. "The life ain't never going out of me!"

"It's because we're growing older," said Sam. "It seems to me that what's happening is that we're all growing towards the time when our life will just leave us." He shrugged his shoulders as puzzled by this as everyone else was.

"When the life goes, the body just crumbles away, doesn't it?" Miriam was crying openly now.

"Well, why hasn't the life left any of us before?" Fortuna wanted to know. While the rest got miserable, she got angry. "We've been here hundreds of years and no life has ever gone before!"

"Because we're different now," said Alice quietly. "Since the No-Life Man came. And there's nothing we can do about it."

Sam looked at them all as they wondered about Martha. He'd discovered something from old Vincente that might help them understand, but he decided not to tell them until everyone arrived. Instead he laid out the paints on the old presses.

"Why don't we make a start with the posters while we're waiting?" he said. "And then we can get the others to help us put them up all over the town."

Slowly, one by one, they took paper and brushes and began to write their own thoughts. Each of them wanted to tell the people of Thistown exactly what they felt.

Fortuna's of course was angry. She wrote in huge bold letters:

WAKE UP THISTOWN!
RASPER IS POISONING YOUR MINDS!
JOIN THE UNDERGROUND!
IT'S YOUR ONLY CHANCE TO STRIKE BACK!

DOWN WITH RASPER!
THROW HIM IN THE CORNFIELDS!!

Sam still didn't really know what to think. His was more forgiving:

We, in the Underground don't wish to lead you.
We only want Thistown to return to the
old days. We wish to forgive Rasper.

And this was Jack Juniper's in his own personal style:

<u>HIT RASPER YEAH!</u>
GET HIM BACK!
DON'T LET HIM GET AWAY WITH IT!
WE WON'T!
WE ARE THE <u>UNDERGROUND!</u>

Miriam was going to repeat her letter to the Opinion, but thought it was too long and Old Martha losing her life had made her wonder about other things. Her poster was more mysterious.

I was free as a bluebird!
I was happy as grass!
Why am I not happy anymore?

Belle's was simple. She'd made seven of them before any of the others had even finished one. It just said:

RASPER IS A RASPBERRY.

Alice didn't make a poster. She couldn't think of what to say. She just sat staring out of the window.

THE SECRET MEETING

They came in the dead of the night. Most of them wore their blue Rasperite uniforms for safety as they crossed the town. They went to the Green, gave a bluebird whistle and Belle collected them and brought them up to the print room. It took over an hour but at last they were all there, except one. For some reason Avenue T Mary hadn't come, but no-one minded, there were enough. After the last one was in they bolted the door.

Miriam and Jack had hung old blankets in the windows and lit the entire room with candles. There were about twelve of them packed excitedly together between the broken presses with the golden glow of the candlelight on their faces. At last something was going to be done about Rasper.

Sam read out the names from his list as he looked round the room: Ray from Avenue X (or X-Ray), Glenn Green (Green Runner because he was so fast), Fortuna Mink, Alice Bright, Miriam Marjorami, Jack Juniper, Tess the Dress, Charcoal Cheryl Black, (Who was brilliant at drawing) Jonny Ridgewood, and the last to come in Baz Brick (As wide as he was tall). And finally Sam Stead himself.

"And me!" shouted Belle, who for some reason Sam had left off the list.

"And Belle," said Sam.

Alice looked along the row of shining, serious faces and felt sure that they would be able to do something about Rasper. She winked at Jonny Ridgewood as Fortuna stood up. She was strong as usual and straight to the point.

"It was my idea to bring us all together," she said, "and I want to say why I did it."

Sam looked to Alice. They both had the same thought. It was certainly Fortuna's idea to bring them together, but she hadn't trudged on her own through the dangerous streets and alleys of Thistown to do it. They'd all done that.

Fortuna went on. "We have come together because we have to act together. Since Rasper took over, Thistown has been in a terrible state. And we have to put it right."

"About time!" shouted X-Ray, tall thin and narrow faced.

"Yeah!" Jack Juniper punched his fist in the air.

"How do we do we get rid of him then?" asked Tess the Dress, small and pale and chewing gum.

"First..." said Fortuna.

"First..." said Sam.

"Wait a minute, Sam." Fortuna thought she was in charge.

"I have something to tell you," said Sam. "We all know this started with the No-Life Man, don't we?" Everyone nodded. "Well, I know where he came from."

JOHN-JOHN

"It makes a lot of difference, you see?" Sam looked round. "When we first saw the No-Life Man at the Hospital, I knew that he reminded me of someone. And today at the Great Hall I realised who it was. It was Vincente Smith, the painter."

"Vincente?" said Alice. "The No-life man didn't look anything like...." She thought for a minute. "Yes he did, didn't he?"

"Yes," said Miriam, "he had the same colour hair...."

"And the same eyes," agreed Tess the Dress."

"Well, what about it?" said Fortuna still standing. She wasn't interested in the No-Life Man. She wanted action to get rid of Rasper.

"But it was more than that," said Sam ignoring Fortuna, "It was the way he looked when he was sad. Both Vincente and the No-life Man had the same kind of sad look in their eyes."

"We don't need this."

"Wait a minute, Fortuna!" Alice snapped. "Sam, what happened?"

"Alice and me went down to the Great Hall to see if we could get some paints for the posters. I went with Vincente into his paint store and asked him if he would help us. He said he'd be happy to because he hated Rasper more than anyone he could ever remember, and most of all he hated painting the picture of the No-Life Man. I asked him why he hated it so much. He didn't want to tell me at first, but I said that the No-Life Man was where it all started and if he could help us understand where he came from then maybe we could do something about it. He looked very sad, and suddenly he said, 'It's all my fault. It's all my fault!' And he began to cry.

Sam's eyes were wide as he spoke. "He told me, it all started with Reggie Run and the Corn Travellers. You remember? When Run thought that when the wind blew in a certain direction it made a path through the corn and if you were quick enough you could get through it to the other side? And hundreds of people believed him and were all gobbled up by the corn?"

Everyone nodded sadly. If there was one story in Thistown that everybody knew, it was that one. They'd all had friends who'd disappeared in the corn. Even Fortuna sat down to listen as Sam went on.

"And do you remember the last woman to leave?"

"Maggie Blush," said Alice. "And she left her hand out, so the corn didn't take it and someone had to throw it back into the corn after her."

"That's right," said Sam. "Well Maggie was Vincente's best friend. He told me that when the Corn Travellers had waited on the Green, he and Maggie had argued over whether to go or not. He didn't want to, but she did. Then he said to me that the whole problem was made worse by John-John."

"Who's John-John?" asked Jack, restless as usual.

"That's what I asked," said Sam. "Vincente started crying again. But after a while he said, 'John-John was my son."

"Son?" asked Alice. "What's that?" They all looked at each other.

"Vincente said that John-John came from him. And came from Maggie as well. They'd made him together. And they thought they shouldn't have done, so they kept him secret."

"How did they make him?" asked Miriam.

"I don't know. He went bright red and wouldn't tell me," said Sam. "And then he said that Maggie wanted to take John-John over the cornfields with her but he said no. They argued and argued. Eventually when the wind blew the path through the corn, Vincente ran back to his house and locked himself in with John-John. Maggie knew that she had to follow the others through the corn at once or it would be too late, so she went and we know what happened to her."

"And what happened to John-John?" asked Fortuna.

"Vincente said he was different from everyone else from the very beginning which is why they kept him hidden."

"How was he different?" asked Tess.

"He was tiny and he kept getting bigger."

"Was he growing?" asked Alice.

"Yes," said Sam, "He was growing. While the rest of us stayed the same age forever, John-John got older every day. He grew from being very small to becoming big and then bigger and then the life left him." He looked round the room, "You see John-John was the No-Life Man."

"How?" several of them asked all at once.

" Well, over all those years as he grew, Vincente kept him in his basement because he was too ashamed to tell us about him." Sam said, "And although Vincente did everything he could to look after him, John-John began to get sickly and pale, because in the basement he never saw the sun, you see?"

"Never saw the sun?" Alice seemed quite upset that such a terrible thing should ever happen to anybody.

Sam carried on, "Then finally one day, he smiled at Vincente, which was the grin that we saw on his face in the hospital, and then the life just left him. Vincente, like the rest of us had never seen a No-Life Man before and didn't know what to do. He panicked and put him in a cart and dumped him in Duster Alley."

"That's why his feet were clean!" said Alice. "We knew he hadn't walked there!"

"That's right," nodded Sam. "So now we know. The No-Life Man is called John-John and was made by Vincente Smith and Maggie Blush. That was the beginning."

"If that was the beginning, what's the end?" asked Alice.

Sam said, "Somehow we must go back to what we were before the No-Life Man came."

"The No-Life Man hasn't got anything to do with it anymore! Our real problem is Rasper!" said Fortuna with an ugly sneer on her face.

Most of them agreed. This what what they wanted to hear.

Jonny Ridgewood was small, but tough enough for anyone twice his size. He stood up and said fiercely, "That's right! Let's get rid of Rasper like he tried to get rid of you!"

"Are you suggesting that we put him in a basement and starve him?" asked Sam.

"Why not?" Fortuna stared at him angrily, "Give me one good reason why we shouldn't?"

"Because it's illegal."

"Because it will make us as bad as Rasper." said Miriam, "And I don't see how that will make Thistown better."

Sam said, "Listen. For the first time in our lives we're all growing, aren't we? My voice is changing. Our cuts won't heal. We're growing up. And that means we're growing towards No-Life. We will all become No-Life people. And that's what we have to stop, isn't it? And the only way to do that is to go back to what we used to be, when there wasn't any No-Life. And we can't do that if we do the same things that Rasper's doing."

"Why not?" asked X- Ray in that strange whine of his.

"Because like Miri said, he's bad," said Sam, "And what we had was good."

"That's all over!" shouted Fortuna.

"That's right." X-Ray agreed.

"The old Thistown has gone forever!" Jack jumped up.

"Rasper's got to go!" yelled Baz Brick, banging his big hand down on a printing press.

"I think he's got to go too!" repeated Tess the Dress.

"How?" asked Alice Bright quietly, "That's what we need to know isn't it?"

"Just like we said before!" Jonny was on his feet again. "Like he did to us!"

"By taking the Life from him!" Fortuna shouted, her eyes blazing.

"No! That's terrible!" Sam stood up.

"Yes! Take the life from him!!" X-Ray shouted.

"Wait! Listen to Sam." Alice pleaded.

Sam said quietly, " Remember. Remember what it used to be like. We never wanted to take the life from anybody before. Why should we now? Because of Rasper? No, we mustn't. We must go back to what we had, and that means *not* being like Rasper. It means *not* doing the things he does. We mustn't take the life from anyone."

There was quiet in the room as everyone considered what Sam had said. As Alice looked round she knew that the others would never agree with him, and much as she wanted to, she didn't think she did either. She knew that what's done is done and that they could never go back. They had to go forward. There was no other way.

Then Miriam said what Alice was thinking, "No, Sam, I'm so sorry." Miriam spoke gently. There were tears glistening in her huge eyes as she said, "Thistown has already changed, you see? It has changed forever."

And that was it. Miriam's simple statement had made up everyone's minds.

Sam sat down slowly. He knew he had lost. He looked at Alice who smiled. Then he looked up at Fortuna.

She stared back at him. "We're going to get Rasper, and that's that." Her face was hard.

"So how do we do it then?" asked X -Ray, twisting his narrow lips.

There was quiet as they all realised the horrible truth. It was all very well for them to get angry and say they were going to get rid of Rasper, but how were they going to do it when there were so few of them and thousands of Rasperites? And as if to show them exactly how awful it all was, there was a sudden hammering at the door.

DISCOVERED

The dreaded foghorn voice of Henry Horne roared from the other side of the door. "We know you're in there! Come on out, before we come in!"

"It's Horne! What do we do now?" whispered Tess.

"Who told them?" Fortuna glared round, "Who's the traitor?"

"It's Avenue T Mary!" said Jack. "That's why she didn't come."

"It doesn't matter about that now," said Alice. "The three of us must get out."

"How do you think we're going to do that?" said Jack.

The banging continued. "Open up! Open up!"

Alice was thinking fast. She turned quickly and said with a smile, "We'll invite them in."

"And be put in the basement?" sneered Fortuna.

"No," whispered Alice quickly. "Listen. Only me, Fortuna and Jack have to hide. They think that the rest of you are on their side. Look, most of you are still in blue uniforms! You could be holding a meeting about anything!" Then in a moment of inspiration she said, "Tell them about the Festival of Sport."

"What Festival of Sport?" asked Sam.

"You'll think of something." said Alice

Henry Horne hammered on the door again, "Open up! Open up! Or we'll break this door down!"

"We're coming," yelled Tess,"

"Quick, get rid of any posters," said Jack.

"Hide! Hide!" said Charcoal Cheryl. "In here."

She opened the long low metal doors of the cupboard beneath one of the smashed machines where the paper rolls had been kept, and the three of them crammed themselves into the low space as the door to the print room began to splinter under the Rasperite hammer blows.

"Alright! I'm coming!" shouted Tess.

She straightened her Rasper blue jacket, unlocked the door, then said to a startled Henry Horne in the politest possible way, "Sorry, we didn't hear you."

Inside the cupboard Alice listened as she heard Horne and the Rasperites stomp into the room and finally thought of the poster she wanted to write.

> **Is it the beginning of the end,**
> **or the end of the beginning?**
> **There's always hope.**

But it was far too late for posters now.

THE GREAT SPORTS EVENT

Horne came straight into the middle of the room with at least a dozen big blue-uniformed Rasperites from Awkward Corner behind him. "And there's another sixty of us on the Green," he shouted, "Just in case any of you are thinking of making a run for it."

"A run for it?" asked Tess the Dress innocently, "Why should we want to do that?"

Horne looked round at the blue uniforms. He was getting confused already. "What are you doing in here?" he shouted.

"I don't think that's any of your business," said Sam.

"Oh, it's you, Sam Stead. We've been watching you."

"Well now you know where I am," said Sam, who had no idea what was going to happen next.

"And her." Horne pointed an ugly finger at Miriam. "What are you up to?"

"You can see for yourself," said Sam pointing at the blue uniforms. "We're having a meeting."

"What for?" shouted Horne. There was a silence as everyone racked their brains thinking of something to tell him.

"It's secret," said Tess sweetly.

"Nothing's secret, Rasper knows everything!" Bill Rory poked his finger in the air.

"Not if it's a surprise for him," Jonny Ridgewood said suddenly.

Nobody knew what he was talking about.

"Surprise?' Horne spat, "What are you talking about?"

Jonny looked round and smiled, "But can you keep the secret? That's the question."

Horne looked a bit worried by this, "What secret?" he asked.

"Shut the door and we'll tell you," said Jonny.

"We're not shutting any door," said Horne. Then he shouted to the Rasperites behind him, "Get them out of here! Arrest them all!"

"Wait a minute." said X-Ray, who was also wearing a blue tunic. "If you want Rasper to be angry with you, that's up to you. But I don't want him to be angry with me."

"We'll tell him what you've done," added Tess.

Horne turned nervously. "What do you mean?"

"She means what she says," said Jonny. "If you want to wreck everything, that's up to you, but don't expect us to take the blame for it."

Horne turned to Rory who didn't know what to say. He turned back and glared, "Alright what is it? And the door stays open!"

"I'm sorry, but we can't tell you," said Jonny. "As I've already mentioned. It's a secret."

"You'll tell us right now , or you're going to the basement!" yelled Horne.

"That's it, the basement!" added Rory, and he produced a long rusty chain, "And we'll lock you to the wall, so no-one will get away again!"

"I hope you're not going to make Rasper angry." said Tess the Dress offering her wrists so that Rory could chain her.

"Why should we make him angry?" Horne wanted to know. "Rory put that chain away, you idiot!" He turned back to Jonny. "Tell us what's going on!"

"Do you swear to keep the secret?" asked Jonny.

"Alright," said Horne unwillingly.

"Do you swear?"

"Alright, I swear!' Horne was beginning to sweat.

"It's quite simple," explained Jonny, making it up as he went along. "It's for the ceremony of the opening the Great Hall. We're going to hold a Supreme Sports Event and Rasperite Rally!"

"Some of these people here, aren't even Rasperites!" shouted Horne, looking nastily at Sam and Miriam.

"Oh yes we are!" yelled back nearly everybody else. The enthusiasm was a bit fake, but it seemed to convince Horne.

"And where's this Sports Event going to be held?" he asked suspiciously.

"In a brand new stadium," said Green Runner thinking quickly. "Obviously I'm doing the racing."

"And I'm doing the throwing," said Baz Brick flexing his muscles. He looked fierce enough to throw Henry Horne out of the room, right there and then.

"I'm making the official's uniforms," said Tess the Dress.

They began to enjoy making it all up on the spot.

"I'm designing the programmes," said Charcoal Cheryl

"And the rest of us are building the Grandstand," said Miriam with her eyes innocently wide open.

"With a special chair for Rasper," said X-Ray.

"Because he will present all the medals." said Jonny.

"Obviously," said Tess.

There was a silence as Horne and Rory tried to take all this in.

"And if you tell Rasper about it, you'll ruin his great surprise," said Tess, still chewing her gum. "So be careful."

"It could be you who ended up in the basement," added Jonny.

Henry Horne and Rory looked at one another, then they went into a huddle in the corner of the room with several other senior Rasperites. Did they believe this or not? At least they weren't searching the place. The three in the cupboard were holding their breath.

After a few minutes Henry Horne turned to face them and said, "The Grand Assembly for the Secret Supreme Sports events will meet here tomorrow night. I will be leader. The rest of you can carry on planning what you plan to do." And with that he walked out and slammed what was left of the door.

Someone giggled, then they all laughed out loud. Horne had believed them!

"And it seems to me," said Alice coming out of the cupboard, "That the Supreme Sports Event would be a very good time to get rid of Rasper, don't you think?"

"Yes!" said Jonny.

And the rest shouted their agreement. The only problem was that if Horne was coming back to the print works, the three who'd been in the goldmine would have to find a new place to hide. But they didn't seem to mind. The Sports Event! Henry Horne breaking into the meeting had given them their plan! That's when they would get Rasper! No-one was really thinking of anything else.

Except for Sam. He still wasn't sure that what they were doing was right. And except for Alice. As she looked around their laughing faces she wondered who it was had told Henry Horne about tonight's meeting. Was it Avenue T Mary who hadn't turned up, or was it one of them here now? And if it was, what else would he or she tell the Rasperites?

FORTUNA'S CELLAR

Fortuna's house was on the Third Circle by Avenue H. Of course the Rasperites had been to her house when they were looking for the Three, but finding nothing, had merely tipped Fortuna's furniture over and left.

At the back of the house were a flight of steps leading down to an old hidden cellar. The three fugitives thought that this would be a perfect place to hide while the Sports Event was being organised. They wouldn't be too far away from what was happening and they could be in touch with Jonny Ridgewood , Tess the Dress and Green Runner who would be the main organisers. Although of course Henry Horne thought he was was the chief organiser, but that was because he didn't know who the real chief was. And there was no doubt about that. It was Fortuna.

If anything her skin was now ever more pale yellow and her hair even blacker. Her sharp, glittering eyes burned with the passion of getting rid of Rasper. It was the only thing she ever thought of. She hardly ate or slept. She prowled the cellar for hour after hour thinking only of taking the life from the tyrant who had destroyed Thistown.

Jack Juniper was always at her side, encouraging her when she was poring over the plans for the event which were spread out on a huge table. Jack agreed with everything she said. Although she wouldn't be able to attend any of the meetings herself because the Rasperites would have arrested her on sight, Fortuna kept in touch with everybody.

One night Sam sneaked through the dark streets and sat with Alice on the floor in the dark living room of the house, leaning on one of Fortuna's broken chairs. He told her about the building of the new stadium. "I don't believe how fast it's all happening," he said.

"It's Fortuna," said Alice. "She gives instructions to Jack who passes them on to Green Runner who comes here about fifty time a day. He takes them to Jonny and Tess on the Events Committee. Then the Committee give the plans to Horne as if they'd made them up themselves. And Horne issues the orders to the carpenters, stonemasons, gardeners and so on. It's quite efficient really."

"It's amazing," said Sam uneasily.

"I don't trust her," said Alice.

"Who?"

"Fortuna."

"I don't trust any of it," said Sam wearily.

"Sam, we've been all through it. There isn't any other way. Rasper is destroying Thistown."

Sam sighed.

"But it's Fortuna I'm worried about," Alice went on. "I think she might be as bad as he is."

"If we do what he does, then we're all as bad as he is," said Sam

Now it was Alice's turn to sigh.

"And what about you?" asked Sam. "What are you doing?"

"I'm working on something else," said Alice quietly.

"Getting rid of Rasper?" He asked.

"Sam, do you really want to know?"

"No," replied Sam sadly.

The two friends were quiet for quite a long time. Sam stared round at the wrecked room and Alice looked at the floor. Somewhere in her heart she knew that Sam was right and they were all becoming just like Rasper. But what else could they do?

"I wonder who it was," Alice suddenly said, "who told Henry Horne about our meeting?"

"It wasn't me, said Sam sadly, "although sometimes I wish I had."

"Oh Sam!" said Alice, "You'd never have done that!"

"I know," he said. "I'm part of it all too, aren't I?"

He got up slowly and wandered back into the night. Sorrowful Sam treading through the darkness. How he wished that Thistown could be like it used to be.

THE GREAT CONSTRUCTION

A few days later, with time weighing heavily on his hands, Sam walked down Avenue A. He stopped, amazed. There in front of him, as if it had grown up out of nothing, stood the huge structure of the new Sports Stadium covered in wooden scaffolding and tarpaulin. Every single carpenter who wasn't working on the Great Hall had been ordered to join the workforce. They worked hard and fast. Carts carried wood from the forest on Avenues P, Q, O and N, and Sam had heard that some of the carpenters had even wanted to cut down the great oaks on the Green.

The Great Hall further down the Avenue still wasn't finished and stone was still being quarried from the Forty-fifth Circle. There seemed to be hammering and nailing and digging and cries of "Timber!" wherever he looked. There were even changes being made to Avenue A itself. It was to be re-named Ronald Rasper Row and decorated with flowers, lights and gigantic ears for the Opening Ceremony of The Great Hall. But by far the biggest task was the building of the Main Grandstand in the stadium. With all the shouts and cries of the workers, the hammering, the sawing, the clattering wheels of the carts, the noise was deafening. Sam looked up. The grandstand seemed so high that it blotted out the sun.

The preparations for the Sports Events themselves were also going ahead rapidly. Horne had meetings with the Events Committee nearly every day. Sam had seen them file into the Opinion building only that morning. He was shocked to see them all dressed in blue tunics, Tess, X-Ray, Glen Green, Baz Brick - even Miriam! But Jonny had given him a re-assuring wink. If he hadn't, Sam might have thought they'd all gone over to Rasper. They were all very thorough. Horne had ordered two factories on Workshop Way to make all the equipment that was need for the various events. Tess was given fifty extra assistants to help with all the uniforms, and Green Runner and Baz where organising the competitions and competitors.

It was all happening so fast and Sam couldn't help but feel a sneaking admiration for all the hard-work and invention of his fellow Thistonians at the same time as feeling a terrible despair that they were doing it for all the wrong reasons. And it was all supposed to be a secret surprise for Rasper! Sam couldn't understand how he didn't know about it. How exactly could he miss it? It didn't take long for him to find out.

"Great Listener Rasper wants to see you."

Sam turned quickly. Bill Rory stood glowering down at him.

"Me?" Sam gulped, "Are you sure you've got the right person?"

"You're Samson Stead, aren't you?" Rory sneered.

"Yes," said Sam. "Why...why does Rasper want to see me?"

"The Great Ear!"

"Sorry, why does the Great Ear want to see me?"

"That's his business. He wants to see you *now*."

THE MAN HIMSELF

'Now?' Rasper was probably the last person Sam wanted to see *ever*, let alone *now*. But before he knew it he was being marched back down Avenue A to Awkward Corner surrounded by Rory and three huge Rasperites with stoney faces. He was shaking. Perhaps there had been a spy at the meeting after all. And perhaps Rasper knew what they were really planning for the Sports Events. Sam with visions of the Town Hall basement racing through his mind, looked ahead to the great oak trees on the Green. Was this the last time he was ever going to see them?

He was pushed roughly into the Peoples' Cafe. It was very different to what it had been the last time he'd seen it with Miriam. All the chairs and tables were gone and it could hardly be called a cafe anymore at all, it was more like a series of meeting rooms or offices. There were huge Rasper posters all over the walls, showing him as the Great Listener, or the Great Ear, and even a painting of the No-Life Man. It was so bad that Sam was sure that Vincente hadn't done it. It was probably Bill Rory, he was bad at everything else, why not painting?

Rory gave him a thump and shoved him into a large and almost empty room at the back. The light was very low but he could make out the shape of a huge chair at one end. This must have been where Rasper was when Alice overheard him speaking to Percy Pike.

"Wait there." said Rory and he immediately disappeared into the gloom at the end of the room.

All Sam really wanted to do was sit down, but didn't dare use the chair at the end. He was sure it was Rasper's and equally sure that the Great Ear wouldn't appreciate one Sam Stead lounging around on his own personal seat. He waited nervously, and after a few minutes a small door opened to one side. He had the shock of his life as Belle walked in.

"Belle?" Sam thought he must be seeing things, "What are you doing here?"

She said, "Don't worry, Sam, it will be alright."

What was she doing with Rasper? Sam could hardly admit the question that raced through his mind. Had Belle been the spy at the meeting? Was it because of her that Henry Horne and the Rasperites had broken in on them? Sam's heart filled with dread at the thought of it.

"Samson Stead!" A mighty voice filled the room. Rasper stomped in through the door dressed in a flowing, bright blue robe. Sam noticed that he had silver glitter in his beard. "Samson Stead! How are you?"

And then to Sam's amazement Rasper shook his hand. First Belle being there, and now Rasper being friendly? This was all getting too much for him. What was going on?

"Sit down! Sit down!" boomed Rasper, "You! Get a stool for Samson!"

Rory hurried out of the dark with a stool as Rasper settled himself into his chair. Sam sat slowly and looked up at the Great Ear. Other Rasperites came in and stood threateningly around the walls.

"Don't look so shocked!" Rasper laughed.

"Belle?" It was all Sam could think of to say.

"Oh it's Belle, is it? Didn't you know she was my favourite?"

Sam turned to look at her. She was standing in the shadows to one side, looking looked down at the floor. So it had been Belle who'd told them about the meeting. What else had she told them? Sam didn't have long to think about it.

Rasper said, "I want to thank you, Samson."

"Do you?" said Sam, having no idea what he was talking about.

"Yes, for the Sports Event." Rasper smirked and then leant forward and held his finger to his mouth, "Ssssshhh!"

And all the Rasperites around the walls did the same thing, "Sssssshhh!" And then they smirked too.

"I know it's supposed to be a great secret, but Belle told me, and I can't tell you how pleased I am, Sam. Apparently you were there yourself? And apparently it was all your idea?"

"W-W-Was it?." stammered Sam. Why would Rasper think it was his idea? Is that what Belle had told him? He looked at her again but she was still staring at the ground.

"Thank you! " Rasper went on. I always thought you were against me, but now I can see that you are a good and loyal Rasperite like the rest of your friends. I'm going to have a blue tunic made for you. And I shall listen out to hear if the No-Life man has anything to say about you." He cupped his hand to his ear, and all the other Rasperites solemnly copied him. Apparently this was the new Rasperite salute. The ear-cup as it became known.

"Thank you," Sam replied, getting more confused by the minute.

"But I want you to do something for me, Samson," Rasper got off his chair and came closer, "Let's not call it the Sports Event, shall we? No. We'll call it the Great Rasper Games! What do you think? Is it a good idea? Yes, I thought you'd like it."

Sam hadn't said a word.

Rasper dropped his head and spoke in a quieter voice, "And the other thing I'd like you to mention is that I've heard the No-Life Man telling me that I'm to present all the medals to all the victorious Rasperites at the Games, because of course only Rasperites will win, and then, listen to this..." Sam listened. "The No-Life Man has told me that there is a plan for me to be carried from the Green to the Great Hall in a chair, which is very good, but I'd like to make a small suggestion, in the utmost secrecy, and of course know nothing about it myself, but I would like it very much if the chair was made of gold." He came so close that Sam could smell his foul breath, "What do you think?"

Sam had no idea what to say. He knew nothing about any chair, gold or otherwise. "Er...yes." he said, staring up at Rasper's ugly mouth which hovered three inches above him.

"Good, very good," He clumped back to his chair very pleased with himself. He could hardly resist clapping his hands together in delight as he said, "Then I shall be out of this dingy dump and live in the Great Hall!"

Rasper was going to live in the Great Hall. So that was his plan. Everybody had thought it had been built in honour of the No-Life Man, but the truth was, everyone had just built Rasper a huge house. All the Rasperites clapped and cheered. They probably thought they were going to be living there too.

"However," continued Rasper, "As we all know, I don't know anything about this. It's all a big surprise."

"Yes, Rasper..er Great Ear," said Sam, beginning to feel a huge relief that he wasn't going to be thrown into the Town Hall basement after all.

"And you'll make sure it all happens just as I've just said, won't you?"

Sam nodded, "Yes, Rasper, er Great...."

"That's it then! Thank you, Samson!" And Rasper got up out of his chair and was gone. The Rasperites in the room immediately followed their leader. The room was empty except for him and Belle. Sam turned slowly to look at her.

She said softly, "The night we went out to find the others for the Underground the Rasperites caught me and told me that if I didn't help them, they'd put me in the Town Hall basement and chain me to the wall and starve me death. That's why I didn't find anyone."

"Oh Belle," said Sam.

"I'm sorry."

"Don't worry about it," Sam turned away. He didn't know what to think. A dozen thoughts raced through his mind. He imagined Belle all alone in the dark, surrounded by towering Rasperites. He imagined how they shouted at her and grabbed her small arms with their big hard hands. He imagined her terror at the thought of being chained up against the hard grey stone of the basement wall and left there to rot. He imagined the sneers and leers of Horne and the other thugs, and he hated them. He turned back to Belle and said, "It's alright Belle, none of us are brave all the time."

"I don't think I've been brave at all."

"And what about taking them food when they were in the Goldmine. That was the bravest thing I've ever heard of."

"I told the Rasperites about the meeting." she said. "But I told them it started an hour later than it did and I thought we'd all be finished by then. But we weren't and so Henry Horne came. But it doesn't matter does it? Rasper doesn't know what the Sports Event is really for."

"He doesn't know that its to..."

"Take his life from him." she quietly finished it for him.

"Is that the truth, Belle?" he asked.

"Yes, it is." She looked at him with tears in her eyes. And he believed her. If anything what she had done had helped them. Rasper believed that the Great Rasper Games were for his glory. Because of Belle he would never think that they were for something else.

"Don't tell the others." said Belle hanging her head again.

"Why did you want me to know?" asked Sam.

"Because....because I had to tell someone."

How could he judge her? He wasn't doing what he believed in either, was he?

"No, I won't tell anyone," he said.

GETTING READY

It wasn't long before the Grandstand was almost complete and the Underground held a final meeting. They all crammed into Fortuna's house so that the goldmine three could attend too. The only ones who seemed to be really important anymore were Fortuna, Jumping Jack Juniper, X-Ray and Tess the Dress. They others were hanging on their every word. Alice and Sam were crushed back against the wall. Everyone except the three and Sam were dressed in bright blue Rasperite uniforms.

"I'd like a final report," said Fortuna.

Jonny Ridgewood stood up, "Henry Horne is so stupid that he believes every word we say!"

There was a blaze of laughter and it seemed as if the blue uniforms all lit up.

Baz Brick said, "And the Grandstand is amazing!"

And Green Runner said, "The running track is the best I've ever seen."

They'd all been working hard and were proud of it. They were laughing and nudging each other as if they'd been Rasperites all their life.

Alice turned to Sam and whispered, "They're so proud of themselves and all they're doing is building for Rasper!"

Sam nodded. As usual he was watching everything and coming to his own conclusions. But he was too scared to speak them anymore.

Avenue X Ray stood up. "You should see the chair we're making. It'll take almost twenty of us to carry it," he said proudly, "It's the biggest chair ever made! And it's gold just like he wanted! Course it'll be mainly us who get the honour of carrying Rasper in it!"

Everybody laughed.

Sam turned towards Alice who was laughing too. The honour? Did X Ray say the honour of carrying Rasper? What was happening? Were they all so in love with their uniforms that they'd become Rasperites now?" He whispered, "Alice why are you laugh....?"

"Address the meeting only!" It was Fortuna glaring at him. "We don't want any whispers, or we'll suspect you're a Rasperite!"

"Sam? A Rasperite!" said Alice indignantly. "Are you joking?"

"He hasn't been helping us, has he?" said Fortuna looking hard at Sam.

He remained quiet. The idea that he had anything to do with the Great Ear was so ridiculous that he didn't have to say anything.

"I think you should take that back," said Jonny. "We may not agree with Sam, but we all know what he's done. And Alice."

There were murmurings of approval and Fortuna said, "Alright, I'll forget it this time." But there was a look in her eye that said she didn't mean it and wouldn't forget it at all. She turned to the rest of them and said, "We can be proud of ourselves, that's all."

RASPER'S PALACE

The day was cold and bright. The last preparations had been going on all night and even now some of the workers were hammering a final nail or raising a last blue flag. Sam and Alice were walking down Avenue C. She was once again disguised as a Rasperite. They looked ahead at the huge Grandstand looming high in the distance.

"It's a shame it's all for Rasper," said Sam, as they walked on.

Alice smiled to herself. Sam still had no idea of what they intended to do.

The first event that day was the Opening Ceremony of the Great Hall. Rasper would be carried in his huge chair from the Green. And after this he'd be carried to the Grandstand for the Games, and then carried back to the Hall for a huge celebration party.

"Can't he walk anywhere?" asked Sam.

"The Great Ear only listens. He doesn't use his feet." said Alice.

Already there were hundreds of people lining the Avenue waiting for the great procession. Most of them had blue flags and there wasn't a house or building that wasn't covered in huge portraits of Rasper as the Great Ear, or that didn't have a Rasperite guard outside.

Sam and Alice pushed through the throng and then cut across the Thirty-third Circle to Avenue A, where they stopped, amazed. Even the size of the Grandstand and the thousands of Rasperites preparing to celebrate hadn't prepared them for the sight of the Great Hall itself. It was a vast stone and wood building covered in gold that shone in the sun. It was not so much a hall as a palace. It made the rest of Thistown look tiny. And as if that wasn't enough, there was a huge tower built on top of it, which supported a huge stone Ear, listening over the Cornfields. All around the base of the ear were huge speakers. When Rasper spoke there wouldn't be a person in Thistown who wouldn't be able to hear.

Sam had been worried that Alice would be recognised, but she had been so insistent on coming that Sam knew that there was more to it than just attending the Games. She hid her face with her hand as she went in through the huge doors of the Hall, but she needn't have bothered. The crowd was so big and the guards so pre-occupied with looking their best for Rasper that no-one would have noticed her anyway.

The first thing they saw was a high platform laid out with blue benches either side of a vast solid gold throne. Above it was the huge window looking out over the cornfields. They turned expecting to see Vincente's painting of the No-Life Man on the East Wall, but instead, to their surprise, they saw a gigantic painting of Rasper instead!

"So Vincente didn't paint the No-Life Man after all," said Sam

"I wish he had. It would be an improvement on that!" said Alice sourly. "Soon there won't be a wall in Thistown that *doesn't* have a picture of him."

"Move back! Move back! To the side there!" yelled a Rasperite as he and several others pushed them all back against the wall.

It was lucky that Alice was tall or she wouldn't have seen anything. There were probably a thousand Thistonians crammed into the vast hall. The crush was so terrible that three people fainted and had to be carried out. Alice was so squashed that she wondered if she wouldn't be next. She was weak with nerves as it was.

Finally there was a blast of trumpets and the town orchestra, or the Rasper Symphonium as it was now called, conducted by the great composer, Philip Note, began the Thistown anthem. A door at the side opened and the senior Rasperites took their places on the blue benches. Henry Horne, Percy Pike, Editor Thrust, Bill Rory and to Alice and Sam's surprise, Tess the Dress and X Ray sat and looked solemnly down on the crowd.

Then there was another huge fanfare from the trumpets and Henry Horne stood and raised his arms. "The Great Ear!" he roared.

As the orchestra swelled Rasper came in dressed in a flowing turquoise robe. He sat on his great throne as more Rasperites came in behind. These were apparently the Great Ear's personal bodyguard. Everyone stood and a great cheer went up as the trumpets blared. Rasper rose and stepped up slowly to the centre of the platform and raised his arms in acknowledgement of the ovation. After what seemed an eternity of noise, he settled back into his throne to begin his speech.

He solemnly thanked the No-Life Man who'd started it all and then spoke as usual of how he was listening to him. "You can't hear him and I can. You don't know the way, and only I can show you..." And so on and so on. By the time he had finished and the crowd had stopped cheering, Alice had a headache.

Then finally came the great chair carried in by at least ten other Rasperite Followers. The chair was gold as Rasper had demanded and was extremely heavy. The Followers slowly lowered it to the ground in front of the the throne. Rasper got up and was helped into the chair.

"From one chair to another," Alice whispered sarcastically.

"Shouldn't you be doing something?' Sam asked.

"Doing what?" asked Alice with a raised eyebrow.

"Nothing," said Sam, looking away. He had no idea what they were going to do to get rid of Rasper, but all the same he was getting as nervous as Alice was. He was beginning to wish he was involved. Anything was better than this waiting. And anyway wasn't it about time he made up his mind? If he didn't think they should take the life from Rasper, shouldn't he tell Rasper? How could he? The Underground were his all friends.

The Rasperites picked up the heavy poles that supported the chair. They carried him grandly to the door of the great hall as the Symphonium played, then slowly up Avenue C towards the Grandstand and the games. The cheers on the Avenue were ear-splitting. They drowned all Sam's agonised thoughts.

THE GREAT RASPER GAMES

There was such a crowd that by the time Alice and Sam got to the stadium the games had started. They stood to one side of the main stand and looked around. All the town was there. Rasper was seated high in the middle of the stand and every now and then a winner of a race or an event would make the long climb up the blue carpeted steps and stand head bowed as the band played and the Great Ear hung a medal round his neck. Editor Thrust leaned forward with his notepad in his hand, writing down every word Rasper uttered.

Sam was getting more than a little bewildered. As every one of the winners approached Rasper for their medal, their faces split into the widest of grins. They seemed pleased and honoured to be close to him.

Even Alice was getting worried. She remembered how all the members of the Underground had looked so proud of their blue uniforms at the meeting in Fortuna's house. Had some of them gone over to Rasper? If they had, then their plan would fail and those who hadn't become Rasperites would be thrown into the basement. She looked at Sam, but as usual these days he seemed sunk in his own thoughts. There was only one thing to do. And she had to do it.

She turned to Sam, "Sam I'm going to...." But she could see he wasn't listening anymore. She slowly edged away from him and disappeared into the crowd, leaving him standing, hollow eyed. He couldn't get it out of his mind. A life was going to be taken. A life was going to be... And he had to stop it. Didn't he? He turned to where he thought Alice was, but saw he was alone. He was in turmoil. What was he to do? All the old arguments were running through his mind as another running race started below him.

At first it looked like it was going to be won by Avenue X Ray, but then Green Runner overtook him and stayed in front, until on the home straight when X Ray went into the lead again and seemed as if he was going to get to the line first. Then with an astonishing last minute burst, Green Runner lived up to his name and streaked through the winning tape with his arms held high.

And then he didn't stop!

Sam stared as he sped towards the grandstand. Sam held his breath as he leapt up to the steps heading fast towards Rasper. Was this it? Was this how they were going to get rid of the Great Ear? Sam could hardly stand it. He didn't know what to do. There were many below Rasper in the Stand who were on their feet, clapping and cheering Green Runner as he flew on up towards the Great Ear. Everyone was standing by now. What was Green Runner going to do? Was he going to take the life from Rasper right there and then? He was taking the steps two at a time. He was going so fast he was almost flying! The great Ear looked down with his mouth open.

He'd never seen anything like it either. Green Runner was only a matter of feet away and Rasper stood uncertainly. Henry Horne started to move in front of his leader to protect him. Other Rasperite bodyguards pushed forward The crowd were screaming, some shouting for Green Runner to stop, others seemed to be egging him on. He skidded to a halt right under Rasper's nose. He looked up at the great sweating face above him and grinned. There was a horrible silence. No-one had any idea of what was going to happen next....

Sam suddenly screamed, *"No!!"*

It was as if his was the only voice in the stadium and it echoed round and round the track and the straining, still faces in the newly built stands.

Nothing moved.

Then Green Runner bowed. It was low and graceful. Sam couldn't believe it. Some Rasperites started to applaud. Green Runner had done it all for Rasper after all. He'd leapt up the steps two at a time just to get to Rasper quicker. None of it was part of any plan to take a life. Green Runner was just showing off!

Several people near to Sam turned to look at him. For a second he thought he was going to arrested, but then someone patted him on the back and said, "Good for you!"

And another said, "Quite understand. It looked as though the Great Ear was in danger there for a minute, didn't it?"

Sam sat down in a daze as Rasper laughed and hung a medal round Green Runner's neck. Sam hardly watched the rest of the events. He somehow knew that there was going to be no attack on Rasper at these Games. And he didn't know how he felt about that. He'd just stood to shout, "No!!" And nothing had happened. Did that mean that Rasper would rule them forever? Is that what Sam wanted?

The competitions came to an end, Rasper made another speech and Sam watched as he was lifted once more into the huge chair to be carried back up Avenue C towards the Great Hall. But this time those that heaved the poles onto their shoulders were all members of the Underground dressed in smart blue tunics. Sam could see that even Alice was one of them. The band marched in front, then behind came the rows and rows of Senior Rasperites and the crowd followed on. The whole of Thistown seemed to be seeing Rasper home to the Great Hall.

The Games had come and gone. The Underground hadn't got rid of Rasper. It even seemed as if they'd joined him. And to Sam that was probably the worst outcome of all. He'd never felt so alone in all his life.

THISTOWN CELEBRATE!

Sam walked slowly back to his house. As far as he was concerned it was all over. He didn't care what happened anymore. What was the point, all his friends had gone over to Rasper. And that even included his very best friend, Alice. He couldn't believe it. He suddenly realised how much he hated Rasper. Maybe he didn't want to take the life from him, but that didn't stop him hating him. He wanted to shout it out and let them come and arrest him and put him in the basement. What difference did it make? Rasper had ruined Thistown. He'd ruined Sam's town! And if there was one thing that Sam definitely wasn't going to do, it was join the crowd again and watch as Rasper, the stupid Great Ear was taken in the golden chair like an emperor into the Great Hall that they'd all built with their own bare hands. And for what? So stupid Rasper who used to be little more than a drunk on Awkward Corner could live in it! No! No thank you! Sam would rather be a No-Life Man himself.

There was a booming from the speakers by the Great Hall, but he couldn't hear what was being said, and he didn't care. He trudged across the Green with his head hung low. He was so despairing and so disgusted that he didn't hear the shouting at first. He only noticed it when he saw two or three Rasperites running across the Green yelling, "Rasper! Rasper!"

Behind them came groups of Townspeople yelling the same thing. "Rasper! Oh Rasper!"

All of them seemed to be running and none of them seemed to know where they were going. "Rasper!" Oh! Oh Rasper!'

Sam turned, bemused. The Green suddenly seemed full of people running in every direction all shouting the same thing. He even saw a Rasperite bawling his eyes out.

"Rasper! Oh Rasper!" The shout was everywhere.

What was happening?

Sam shouted at Detective Willis who ran past him with his great fat cheeks wet with tears. "Flouncy! Sergeant Willis...."

But all Willis could do was bellow, "Rasper! My Rasper!" and then he ran on like a headless chicken, going in pointless circles round the great oaks.

Even the bluebirds seemed to have joined in. They were squawking madly as they flew round the trees in great swirling swarms.

Then came Nurse Pine.

"What is it?" asked Sam.

She just stared back at him. She was in a state of shock, her mouth opened and then closed and then she wandered on, stumbling over the grass.

At last Sam saw the doctors, Stitch and Slice. He thought he'd get some sense at last.

"Doctor Stitch? Doctor Slice?" They stopped and stared at him. "What's happened?"

"Er.."

"Um?"

"Can't you tell me?"

"It's..."

"Well.."

Then they both spoke together. "!t's unbelievable!"

Sam was beginning to think he would never get a sensible answer from anyone when suddenly a voice came booming out of the loudspeakers near to him.

"People of Thistown!"

It was so crackly and loud that it was difficult to make out whose voice it was. Everyone stopped dead in their tracks. Willis held his head with its his tear-stained cheeks up to the speakers, Nurse Pine stopped stumbling, and the two doctors stopped mumbling. Everyone stood stock still.

"People of Thistown!" The voice through the Speakers boomed. " Celebrate! Rasper's gone. Thistown Celebrate! *Rasper's gone!*""

Nurse Pine fainted. Flouncy bawled. And then Sam saw the two doctors turn to one another and slowly smile.

Rasper's gone? What had happened?

The voice said again, *"Celebrate!"*

And it was only then that Sam recognised the voice as Fortuna's. He'd hardly got over the shock when Alice came running up with the biggest, broadest, beamiest smile he had ever seen. She jumped high into the air and yelled, "Haven't you heard? *He's Gone!*"

RASPER FLIES

Alice sat Sam down under a great oak, then jumped up again herself because she was far too excited to keep still when she had so much to tell him.

"We did it!" she yelled and threw her arms in the air again.

"I know you did it," said Sam. "I want to know *how!*"

"He said could hear the voice of the No-Life Man over the cornfields, didn't he? Well he definitely can now!" Alice laughed.

Sam sighed. Would he ever get the story of what had happened?

"Alright," said Alice, and she knelt down in front of him. And then she jumped up again.

"Alice!"

"Sorry." She knelt down again. "You know when I left you in the stadium?"

"And didn't say goodbye," said Sam.

"Well, that's not surprising. You were hardly talking at all, were you?"

"I suppose not."

"And anyway, I didn't think you wanted to know what we were going to do."

"What *did* you do, Alice?" said Sam exasperated by now.

"You see when we stood in the stadium together and saw everyone in their uniforms, I thought, like you probably did, that they'd all gone over to Rasper."

"I wasn't thinking anything much," said Sam.

"Anyway I decided to go and see what was going on, and if there was anybody who was thinking of changing their minds then they would have to tell me to my face. I was about to tell Tess the Dress exactly what I thought about it all when..." Alice's unusually fierce face broke into a smile, ".... I saw Green Runner bounding up the steps towards Rasper. And I knew everything was alright. You see Green Runner was part of the plan! We knew that everybody would get worried for a second and think that he was going to do something right there and then. And Horne and Rory would panic, and run towards Rasper and that would give us all the time to slip away without anybody noticing. And that's exactly what happened."

"Where did you slip away too?" asked Sam

"Well, if you'll give me a chance, I'll tell you." said Alice. "We all met by the great golden chair. *We* had to get their first, you see, to make sure that it was us that carried the chair and not any of his followers. Fortuna and Jack were there in disguise. She does look good in a uniform, I have to say...

"Alice!"

"Alright. All of us, all the Underground, we lined up by the chair waiting for Rasper so that we could carry him from the games back to the Great Hall."

"What did you want to do that for?"

"Will you shut-up, please?"

"Sorry."

"Anyway, the problem was that the Rasperite Followers of course thought that they should carry the chair, but Jonny Ridgewood was brilliant. He stepped up to Pike who was supposed to be the lead carrier and said, 'Mayor Pike, I have to congratulate you. I have just had a message sent down from the Great Ear himself. You and all the first chair carriers are to be promoted. And you, Mayor Pike are to be promoted especially. You are to be made the Great Ear's Aide!'

We all thought this was very funny, but of course Pike didn't get it because as we all know his skull's about a foot thick, and he hopped about in ecstasy saying how he was going to be a hearing Aide!

Jonny said, 'And all the rest of you will be junior Ear-Aides in honour of your carrying the chair the first time. And you're all to go straight to the Town Hall to be fitted with special Ear-Aide uniforms and be given medals and special scrolls in a great ceremony when His Honour Rasper the Great Ear is carried in by the rest of us. After all it wouldn't do to be presented with an award when you were all hot and sweaty from carrying a chair, would it?'

'No, it certainly wouldn't!' said Pike.'

'Well get a move on,' said Jonny, 'You're uniforms are waiting!"

'Yes! Yes!' said Pike. 'Did you say a great ceremony?'

'With the town orchestra playing.' said Jonny with his eyes wide.

And we all started clapping as though Pike was the greatest man in Thistown, and off he went up to the Town Hall to put on a uniform that didn't exist."

"That's so typical of Pike, isn't it?" said Sam. "He thinks he knows everything and he really knows nothing."

"And so," said Alice, "we all took up our positions around the chair and it wasn't too long before there was a great cheer from the stadium and then there was Rasper marching down towards us with his Rasperites. The three of us who were in disguise kept our heads right down and no-one noticed us as Henry Horne and Bill Rory helped Rasper up into the chair, which was very heavy, let me tell you. Who designed it? Whoever it was, I'm going to have a word."

"Alice!"

"Alright, Alright. So we started to carry the chair towards the Great Hall. And the Town band formed up behind us and started to play that terrible song written by composer, Note." Alice stood up and sang it out.

Oh Rasper, Oh Great Ear!

Lead us from our fear!

Several people on the Green turned to watch and Alice sat down again quickly. She went on, "And the crowds we marched past were waving their pictures of the Great Ear and cheering. The Rasperites behind were singing with all their hearts as the band played. And Rasper waved back with a huge, horrible grin on his face. He was so happy. Everyone adored him and everything was just as he could ever have wanted."

Sam listened his eyes wide.

"We marched and marched, and the chair seemed to get heavier and heavier, but at last the Great Hall was in sight in front of us.

'Now!' said Jack Juniper who was in front with X Ray. And we all started to go a bit faster. And the band behind us had to go a bit faster, and so they played faster, and everyone sang faster!

"Rasper, Oh Great Ear! Rasper, Oh Great Ear!"

And then we went even faster, and the band played even faster, and everyone sang faster!

"RasperOhGreatEar! RasperOhGreatEar!"

And then we got even faster and the chair started to wobble.

And Henry Horne shouted out. "Don't drop him!"

And Jack shouted back, 'Not yet!'

And we went even faster, and so did the band, and by now the song was so quick it was sounding ridiculous;

"Rasperogreatyeh! Asprogreatyeh! Asprogreyeh!"

And we were coming up towards the doors of the Great Hall which were slowly opening to receive us, and we were going so fast, we were running full pelt with the chair on our shoulders, and by now the band were playing so fast that it didn't sound like music at all, just like a big trumpet scream, and the song was just;

"ASPROYEH! ASPROYEH!"

And as we came up to the doors yawning to meet us, we didn't go through but turned suddenly LEFT!"

"Left?" said Sam.

"And because the band behind were going so fast and didn't know we were turning left, they carried on straight ahead, and those in the front tripped up on the Great Hall steps, and those in the middle tripped up on those in front, and those in the back tripped up on those in the middle, and the Rasperites behind, including Horne and Rory, tripped over all of them. All that was left of the procession was a great pile of heaving, kicking bandsmen and Rasperites! "

"And what happened to the chair?" asked Sam

"We'd gone round the Hall!" said Alice, "And you know where that leads don't you?"

"To the Cornfields." said Sam, his eyes wide.

"To the *corn!*" Shouted Alice brimming over with the excitement of it all. "By now no-one could stop us. Rasper was in his chair and he could see what was coming.

He started screaming, 'Stop! Stop! Someone stop them!'

But it was too late. And anyway, no-one knew what was happening. They probably thought that Rasper, the chair and all of us were going to disappear forever into the yellow! But we didn't, because we had it all planned. When we were only a few feet from the Corn, Jack and X Ray at the front suddenly dug their heels into the road at the same time as they dropped their poles! So the front of the chair came down into the ground just a foot away from the corn as they leapt out of the way, and at the back all the rest of us heaved upwards and the chair went flying up into the air, and Rasper shot out of it like a stone out of a catapult! And then....And then..." Alice stopped as she saw it all again, "And then Rasper flew though the air. He seemed to be up there for ages! We all stood rooted to the spot, we couldn't even breath.

We heard him shout, 'NO!!! I AM THE GREAT EAR......!

And then there was no sound at all as he went lower and lower and suddenly....nothing. He was gone. He'd gone into the corn, Sam. There was no Rasper anymore. Just corn." Alice's eyes were brimming over with tears. "No Rasper, Just corn."

Sam didn't know what to say. It seemed that Rasper really had gone. Years before he'd lost one leg in the corn, and now it had taken the rest of him.

FORTUNA SPEAKS

"Of course all the Rasperites behind us couldn't believe it," said Alice. Their great leader was gone. They were as shocked as we were, but that didn't last long. Horne and Rory were in a fury.

"They shouted 'Get them! Throw them into the corn!!"

And they started to come towards us. We didn't know what to do. There was nowhere to run and there were hundreds of them, but then...then there was a voice from the Great Hall speakers!

It said, 'The Corn has spoken! The Corn has spoken!'

And everyone stood still. I knew who the voice was. It was Fortuna. And that's what I mean when I said, I don't know *how* it happened. I know she was with us carrying the chair when we were at the stadium. She must have slipped away when we were running and somehow got into the Great Hall to the microphone. And now she was telling us that the Corn has spoken.

And then she said with her voice booming out through the speakers, 'Rasper is gone. Down with Rasper! *Down with Rasper!*"

And suddenly everybody was running. Henry Horne and Rory just stood there as all the Rasperites began to panic without their leader. And anyway perhaps the corn had really spoken and taken Rasper. And maybe it would come after them next. And what about the rest of the people? What would they think? Everybody really knew that Rasper was hated, although everybody said the opposite. So what would the people do to the Rasperites, like Henry Horne and Bill Rory? They didn't wait to find out. They just ran away. Just like that, Sam. They ran away!"

Suddenly the speakers on the Green boomed out. It was Fortuna again.

"Thistown Celebrate!"

She must have got all the town's speakers hooked into her microphone now," said Sam.

"Rasper's gone forever! We will never have a leader like him again!" shouted Fortuna.

"Never have a leader like him again?" said Sam in surprise.

"Certainly not," said Alice.

"I was hoping that we'd never have another leader *at all*." said Sam.

Then they heard the first shouts. "Down with Rasper! Down with Rasper!" It was people from the crowd who'd run up from the Great Hall to the Green and who only minutes ago had been cheering him.

Sam and Alice stood and looked around. They couldn't believe it. Some Rasperites were already tearing off their blue uniforms and throwing them on the ground. "Down with Rasper!" Down with Rasper!"

And soon it was a roar. It was as if the whole town was shouting with one voice,"*Down with Rasper!*"

ANOTHER LEADER

Alice went home happy for the first time in many weeks. Sam wasn't so sure that things had changed for the better. He lay tossing and turning in his bed. There were too many things to think about. Rasper was gone, so what would be next? He couldn't get out of his mind Fortuna saying, "We'll never have another leader like him again?" So who was to be the next leader? It wasn't long before he found out.

There was a knock on his door the next morning. It was Alice. Sam was grumpily making his tea when she thrust a poster under his nose.

"Look! They're all over the town!"

Sam fumbled for his glasses in his dressing gown pocket.

"I'll read it to you," said Alice impatiently. "It says, *Emergency Meeting of the Town Assembly. Fortuna will speak.*"

"Fortuna will speak!" Sam woke up quickly. "Why is she speaking to the Town Assembly?"

"And who organised all these posters?" asked Alice.

"It must have been her."

"So why does she think she can call a meeting of the Town Assembly?"

"Because..." Sam didn't finish. He knew why.

"Because she thinks she is going to be the next leader. That's why," said Alice for him.

"We never had leaders before," said Sam unhappily.

"Are you going to pour me a cup of tea? I haven't had any breakfast." Alice sat at the table. "And there's been another No-Life Man."

"Who?" asked Sam, pouring tea down his dressing gown

"it's the composer, Philip Note," said Alice. "Stitch or Slice told me this morning. He'd been drunk at the People's cafe and there'd been a lot of arguing and he'd been shouting a lot.....and...." she stopped.

"What happened?" said Sam from behind the glasses he'd finally found on the kitchen table.

"Someone stuck a knife in him."

"Someone stuck a...." Now it was Sam's turn to stop talking.

They were both very shocked. Nothing like that had ever happened before in Thistown.

"And the life went out of him," said Alice. "It was done on purpose too. They took him to the Hospital, but there was nothing the doctors could do. The life was already gone."

Sam sat opposite Alice at the table. "Poor old Note." he said.

Alice was close to tears, "It's terrible. I thought all this No-Life business would be over once Rasper was gone"

"I think No-Life is with us forever, " said Sam. "It started when Vincente Smith and Maggie Blush made John-John and now it's with us always."

AN UNDERGROUND SPLIT

The first thing that Sam and Alice saw when they took their seats in the public gallery for the meeting was that all of Rasper's old assembly had been replaced by members of the Underground. Avenue X Ray, Green Runner, Tess the Dress, and Baz Brick were sitting round the table.

"It's alright," said Alice, "It's all the old Underground."

"Why didn't anyone ask you and me?" asked Sam disconsolately.

"Well, perhaps they couldn't find us." said Alice.

"Or they didn't look. And who did the asking anyway?"

Sam's question was answered by Fortuna who swept in to the room with Jack Juniper and Percy Pike behind her. She sat down in a chair at the head of the table and said, "Alright Pike, you can sit there. You're the only Rasperite we're allowing. And that's only because you were on the Assembly before."

"He's only there so the rest of the town won't think it's only her friends on the Assembly." said Alice. "Fortuna must have been working on this all night."

"She doesn't sleep anymore," said Miriam who slipped into a seat behind them with Jonny Ridgewood.

"Neither of you were asked either?" asked Sam looking round.

They shook their heads.

"It looks as though Fortuna's made up her mind who her friends are," said Sam.

"And it's not us," said Jonny.

Alice said, "She can't do that. I've had enough of this." She stood up and shouted down into the hall, "Who says all these new people should be on the assembly? Who elected....?"

Fortuna cut her off, "The New Assembly has been sworn in. Hasn't it, Pike?"

"Oh yes, and very good it is too." Pike said greasily.

"But why should it only be your favourites?" Alice shouted.

Fortuna stared at up her, her almond eyes flashing. "It was an emergency. The old Members were Rasperites. They retired. Isn't that so, Pike?"

"Oh, yes. They retired to make way for someone better." He bowed towards Fortuna.

She turned away from him in disgust and then looked angrily back up to the gallery, "And we'll have no more interruptions from you up there, or you'll be removed."

"You can't remove us," Alice shouted down, "We have a right to be here!"

X Ray stood up quickly from the table. He leaned back with his long body and sneered up at them, "The Head of the Assembly has said you'll be removed an' you will. So shut up!"

Alice was too shocked to reply.

"Thank you," said Fortuna. "Now the first of the days business.

X Ray remained standing and spoke, "Last night, Philip Note, the great composer became the latest No-Life Man. He had a knife stuck in him. We know who did it and so we arrested them and chucked them in the cornfields."

This was too much for Alice. She stood again, "You did what?" she erupted.

"I told you what we did." snarled X Ray.

"You threw them in the Corn!"

"Yeah, and they disappeared!"

There was scornful laughter round the table. Alice couldn't believe that Tess the Dress was smirking at someone disappearing."

"And who were they?" Alice wanted to know.

"Henry Horne and Bill Rory!" There was more laughter from the table.

"They struggled, I can tell you that!" X Ray laughed.

"But we were too strong for 'em." shouted Baz Brick raising his muscular arms.

"Henry Horne and Bill Rory!" Alice couldn't believe it. "You didn't throw them in the cornfields because they'd stuck a knife in Note! You threw them in the cornfields because they were Rasperites, and they were your enemies!"

"Look what they'd done to Thistown," said Fortuna calmly. "They deserved it."

Sam suddenly stood, "You're as bad as they were!"

"Oh dear," said Fortuna. "It looks as if the Assembly will have to go into private session."

"You can't do that!" shouted Jonny Ridgewood getting as angry as everyone else. "The Assembly is always public so that we can all see what's going on!"

"Well, now it's not public anymore, is it?" said Fortuna as though she was bored. "You can hear what I have to say on the Green tonight when I address the rest of the town." Then she yawned, "Get rid of them."

"No!" shouted Alice.

Jack Juniper stood up and said calmly, "Clear the gallery."

"That's it!" yelled X-Ray.

"Get them out!" shouted Baz Brick Boy.

And suddenly six big men who had previously been Rasperite guards appeared in the gallery and looked threateningly at Sam, Alice, Jonny and Miriam.

"Now will you go?" said Fortuna sweetly as she flicked a piece of fluff from her jacket. "I do so hate violence."

"Come on," said Sam. "What's the point? We've seen what they're like, and what they'll do."

He walked up to the guards and waited patiently until they moved aside to give him room to walk through the door. The others slowly followed as the Assembly down at the table booed and jeered.

"Bye Sam," yelled X Ray. "You should have been with us, shouldn't you?"

"Not very bright, Alice?" shouted someone else.

"Back to the ridge, Jonny!"

"Is it magic, Miriam, or what?"

The four of them left the gallery and stood outside the Town Hall. No-one knew what to say. Fortuna had betrayed them. Now it seemed as though she was as bad as Rasper ever was. The Underground were no longer together. The strength that could have saved Thistown had been split in two.

"Even Jack Juniper," said Alice. "He came down to the goldmine with us."

"So did Fortuna," said Sam sadly, "and look what's happened to her.

"And now there's only us," said Miriam. "Just four."

IN THE PINK

They met again that night in the old Opinion office.

"Where's Mr Pen?" said Alice looking round.

"He doesn't come out of his house any more," said Miriam. "He can't walk because of his back and he thinks the life will go from him soon."

Alice turned sadly away. Even now they all hoped that it would all somehow be different and that they had misjudged Fortuna. But the moment they looked out of the windows and saw a crowd gathering under the lights to listen to Fortuna and huge Pink banners hanging down from the balcony of the Town Hall, they knew nothing had changed.

"They burnt all the blue Rasper uniforms in a big bonfire on the Green this afternoon," said Miriam. "Fortuna's colour is Pink."

"And there's pictures of her stuck to every tree," said Sam despairingly.

Most of the town had gathered below, but there was no excitement. Everybody else seemed to know that Fortuna wasn't going to change things much. It was all going to be the same as Rasper. Even the police around the crowd were the same. The Four sat by the windows. They'd seen it all before. Somehow they knew it was the beginning of the end for Thistown.

The first to appear on the balcony was Pike, after him came the new Assembly, all dressed in Pink uniforms. Pike went up to the microphone and pulled an important face. "People of Thistown…

"Guess what's coming next?" whispered Alice.

"Fortuna Mink!" roared Pike.

The Town band played the anthem and Fortuna swept onto the balcony dressed in a huge, flowing pink robe. She was followed as usual by Jack Juniper, who now seemed to be her personal bodyguard. She went up to the microphone and said sweetly, "People of Thistown…"

"Guess what's coming next?" whispered Alice again.

"I am the new Great Ear!" said Fortuna

The police and several Fortuna Followers started to clap and looked round to make sure that everyone else did too.

Fortuna went on, "Rasper was a cheat. He couldn't hear over the cornfields. But I can! The No-Life Man will speak to me. He already has! He showed me how to defeat Rasper!"

The crowd on the Green began to applaud again. This time it was louder as though they had begun to accept the inevitable.

Sam turned away. "I can't stand anymore of this."

They turned away from the Green to leave Fortuna to make the speech that Rasper would have made. She went on, and on, and on.

"This is where we all met at the beginning," said Alice sadly looking around at the old printing presses.

"Where we did the posters," said Miriam.

"We can't do all that again." said Alice.

"But we've got to get rid of her!" Jonny banged his hand on a table.

"What's the point?" said Sam. "There'll just be someone else standing up there on the balcony instead of her. They'll just have a different colour uniform on."

"What's it going to be next?" asked Miriam, "Purple with yellow spots?"

"I suppose we'll always have a leader from now on." said Alice, depressed at the thought.

"Yes," said Sam dejectedly, "And I think we'll always have No-Life People too.

"Once it's started, it never stops." said Miriam.

"We have to get out of here," said Sam.

"How?" said Jonny.

"There's only one way. The cornfields."

"Oh yeah," said Jonny. "What shall we do, fly? Let's face it, we can't try the corn again. Look what happened to the Corn Travellers. Look what happened to Rasper."

"You're right, we can't go *through* the corn," said Sam looking up at them.

"What then?" asked Alice.

"But we could try under the corn."

"You mean dig a tunnel for a million miles?" asked Jonny.

"Maybe we won't have to," said Sam.

"Sam, what *are* you talking about?" said Alice.

"Near where you were in the goldmine there was an underground lake."

"What about it?"

"I noticed there was a channel that went down under the rock." Sam went on. "And the water flowed into it. It must have been flowing somewhere."

"Where?" asked Jonny.

Sam shrugged his shoulders. "We could find out."

"There was an old boat!" said Alice, suddenly getting excited by the idea.

"But we don't know for sure, do we?" said Miriam, not so keen, "It sounds more dangerous than living here."

"Going into an underground tunnel, is pretty scary," said Jonny.

"Fortuna might turn out to be a very good leader," suggested Miriam.

It was amazing how their opinion of Fortuna had changed since the idea of going down a dark underground channel had been mentioned. But it's equally amazing how things can change again. There was the pounding of footsteps on the stairs, the door burst open and Belle came bounding in. She was breathless, her eyes were wild with fear and she waved her arms unhappily as she panted, "You've got to get out! You have to! Quick!"

Everyone looked at her. "Hurry! While Fortuna was speaking....in the Clarion offices...Thrust was there....he helped them....They used the Clarion presses....it must have been because of what you did in the Town Hall this morning! Fortuna's furious!"

"What?" asked Alice. "What's happened?"

"This!" shouted Belle. "They're putting them up all over the place. Right now!" She spread a crumpled poster out on top of one the old presses. "Look! It's you! *Again!*" It was a wanted Poster. They couldn't believe it. It said:

**SAMSON STEAD. ALICE BRIGHT
MIRIAM MARJORAMI. JONNY
RIDGEWOOD**

Dangerous criminals!
WANTED FOR TREASON
Contact Thistown Police with any knowledge of their whereabouts. A reward will be given for information leading to the capture of any or all of them, life or No-Life.

They couldn't believe it.

"Dangerous Criminals! I'm not a dangerous criminal!" Jonny exploded.

"What are we supposed to have done?" asked Alice.

"They're saying you're planning to get Fortuna." said Belle.

"Well, we thought about it," said Jonny, "Sure, but we didn't do anything!"

"What's this?" said Alice looking down at the paper. *"A reward will be given for information leading to the capture of any or all of them, Life or No-Life."* She looked around at them, "What does that mean?"

There was a horrible silence. They all knew what it meant.

"It's like when someone put a knife into Note," said Miriam, very frightened. "That's what they're saying people can do to us. And get a reward."

"Why does Fortuna hate us so much?" Alice couldn't believe it. "She was one of us. One of the Underground"

"Not any more," said Belle, "They're all called 'Fortunates' now, after her. You can't say Underground now. The Underground is banned."

"Why?" asked Alice.

"Because the Underground is dangerous. That's what she says anyway."

"Dangerous!" Alice exclaimed, "I'll show her who's dangerous!"

"You haven't got time!" said Belle, "They know you sometimes come here. She has her own Rasperites now. They're called the Fortunate Guard."

"The Fortunate Guard?" Sam couldn't believe it.

"They're her own personal police," said Belle. "She's given X Ray a brand new black uniform, and he's got loads of Fortunate Guards, all in black."

"We have to go," said Sam, "The Goldmine."

"Fortuna knows about it," said Miriam. "She was there with us.

"Look!" said Jonny.

He was pointing down to the Green. In all the excitement of this terrible news they hadn't noticed that Fortuna's speech was over and the meeting below had finished. And now striding towards the Opinion Building was X Ray with at least twenty others behind him, all dressed in black.

"There's Jack Juniper and Baz Brick!" said Jonny

"And they're coming here!" said Miriam.

"Let's get out of the back!" shouted Jonny.

"Thanks Belle." said Sam turning to her, "I want you to know that I think you're the bravest...."

"I'm coming too," she shouted. "There's not four of you, now there's five!"

CHASED BY X-RAY

They left the building and ran quickly onto Workshop Way. The factories were closed down for the night and rose high above them, dark and deserted, as they went quickly past.

"Through here," said Sam and he ran through a tiny gap between two huge dark walls.

"It's Duster Alley," panted Belle, "where we found the first No-Life Man."

"It's too late to think about that now," said Alice. "Come on."

They came out of the alley and turned left onto the Third Circle and kept going until they reached Avenue R. From there they could see back to the Green.

"No-one's coming after us yet," said Sam. "They must still be searching the Opinion building."

"We'll go straight up the Avenue then," said Alice. "It's the quickest way."

So they began the long journey towards the old goldmine. They could see the great wheel of the lift rising out of the darkness far ahead of them.

"We'll never get there in time!" Miriam was already breathless.

"Yes, we will," said Sam.

Alice had never seen him look so determined.

"We won't run. We'll walk as quickly as we can, and get into a rhythm."

And that's exactly what they did. They took big fast strides with Sam in the lead, then Alice, followed by Miriam and Jonny, with Belle having to run behind because her legs weren't long enough for their huge steps. After a while they heard shouts, and looking back they could see the Fortunate Guard gathering in the distant low lights behind them on the Green.

"Just keep going as we are. We'll have enough time," said Sam gasping for breath.

"Just imagine Flouncy Willis bobbling along behind us," said Alice. "I doubt if he'll even get as far as the Fourth Circle!"

"Save your breath for walking," said Sam as they strode on up past the Twentieth Circle, then the the Twenty-first, and then.... soon they'd stopped counting and just concentrated on keeping their legs going. And all the time they could hear the shouts of the Guard behind them.

Miriam suddenly panicked. "Supposing the boat's got a leak?"

"That's a risk we'll have to take," said Sam.

"But suppose they catch us and stick knives into us!"

"Then we'll find out what No-Life is, won't we?" said Jonny, his strong little legs pounding along the Avenue.

By the time they'd reached the Thirty-fifth circle they could see the vast darkness of the Edge and the cornfields ahead of them.

"We'll never be able to get across them," said Miriam.

"We're not going to cross them, we're going under them," said Alice.

"If the boat doesn't leak!"

"Well you can always wait here for X Ray," said Jonny.

Miriam glanced back. She could see the torches of the Fortunate Guard behind them. "No! I'm coming with you!" she said. And ran to catch them up.

DOWN THE MINE AGAIN

"Here! It's here," said Belle, and she led them again to the hole in the fence. They squeezed through one by one and were once again in the huge yard of the goldmine.

"We'll take the lift and leave it down," said Alice. "They'll have to wait for it to come up again, won't they?"

"We could jam it when we get out of it," said Sam. "Then they won't be able to bring it up."

"Yes!" said Alice. "Excellent!"

Sam's idea cheered them up, and they all piled into the ancient lift and pulled the lever for it to descend.

"How will you jam it?" said Miriam when they'd reached the bottom.

"We have to make sure the door stays open," said Sam. "And then it won't go up again."

"Here!" said Jonny who was struggling with a huge piece of old timber.

"That's it!"

They all ran to help and soon had the timber jammed in the door of the lift.

"That'll never close now," said Sam.

"They'll have to climb down the way I used to," said Belle. "It'll take them ages!"

In better spirits now, they started off down the tunnel.

"It's down hill," said Sam. "Find two carts."

"If we push the rest down, they won't be able to use those either!" said Alice.

There weren't too many carts left as Belle in all her various journeys to the top for food had pushed most of them to the bottom of the tunnel. But those that were there they shoved down the track until they heard them rumble away into the darkness on their own. Them they jumped into the last two. Sam pushed the first, and Jonny the second, then they jumped in as they started to gather speed. Soon they were hurtling down through the darkness towards their old cave.

"Look out!" shouted Belle in the front cart.

And it was lucky she did, because the cart suddenly came to an abrupt halt at the end of the track, the second cart stopped dead behind and Alice fell out of it.

"Alice!" shouted Sam. "Are you alright?"

"Yes," said Alice, "but it's pitch black. We can't see each other."

"We left some candles in the cave." said Miriam out of the darkness.

"How do we get to the cave if we can't see where we're going?" asked Jonny.

"I'll show you," said Belle, the darkness making her whisper for some reason. "I've done this journey so many times I could do it blindfold. Take my hand."

They all groped for one another's hands in the dark and followed Belle into the tiny tunnel. Sam thought that this time was worse than the last and was sure that his knees were bleeding. Miriam hated it again. But Alice didn't mind too much. She didn't like the bruising and the water dripping down on her back, but she quite liked the dark. It made her feel secure in a strange kind of way.

They crawled along, too breathless to talk, and after what seemed an age, the tunnel began to get bigger and bigger.

"You can probably stand up now," said Belle.

"Ouch!" said Sam as he'd stood too quickly and banged his head. He walked on with his head bowed until he felt he could straighten up.

As soon she felt as though they were out of the tunnel Belle said, "Wait here, I'll get the candles."

She groped her way forward and left them standing in the pitch black. They couldn't even see their hands in front of their faces.

"What was that?" said Jonny.

"What?" said Alice, jumpily.

"I thought I heard something."

"The Fortunate Guard?" Miriam was beginning to panic again. Ever since Jonny had suggested that she wait for X Ray, her mind had been full of wild imaginings of being chained to the wall in the Town Hall basement.

"Maybe it was nothing," whispered Alice.

But just the thought had made them all jumpy and they were overjoyed when they saw the faint glow of a candle slowly emerging from the darkness ahead of them.

"We left a whole box full of candles," said Belle, and matches," and she rattled a couple of boxes to prove it. "But there wasn't much food." She dropped a small bag at her feet.

"Never mind. Take a candle each," said Sam, "and we'll find the boat."

THE UNDERGROUND RIVER

It was good to see each others faces again as they lit the candles, although they were surprised to see how serious they all looked. Sam seemed very concerned, Jonny was twitching with worry, Miriam's huge eyes shone in the light as she looked around carefully and only Alice seemed to have the same old sparkle.

They found to their surprise that were standing almost next to the underground lake. It stretched away from them beneath the rocks, shimmering in the candlelight.

"There's the boat!" said Alice.

They stumbled over the rocks towards it.

"Does it leak?" Asked Miriam, getting worried again.

"It doesn't look like it," said Sam, "but we won't really know until we're out on the lake in it."

"Oh no! I can't swim."

"I'll rescue you, Miri," said Jonny. "I swim in the river up on the ridge every day."

"Thank you, Jonny."

"It won't sink," said Alice getting into the boat.

"How do you know?" asked Miriam, following her.

"I don't," said Alice. "But I'm going to start believing that things will be alright, and I think the rest of you should do the same."

"Alright, I believe," said Jonny getting in. The boat rocked in the water. He laughed and said, "No I don't!"

"Push it away from the rocks," said Sam, once they were all in. "Who'll take the oars?"

"Me." said Alice.

"And me," said Jonny.

"What's that?" Miriam shouted and then made it sound like a whisper.

There'd been a definite crash from somewhere in the darkness behind them.

"It's the guard trying to get the lift to work," said Sam. "Don't worry, by the time they realise it'll never work and that they have to climb down, they'll be hours behind us."

"Well row then," said Miriam. "Let's see if we can get under the cornfields."

Sam pushed them away from the rocks and Alice and Jonny started to row.

"See, it doesn't leak. What did I tell you? You just have to believe that's all!"

"Row, Alice," said Sam.

And she did. No-one spoke. The water was a deep black reflecting back their faces in the candlelight. Soon they couldn't hear the guard anymore. It was quieter than they'd ever known. Great dark rocks loomed either side of them flickering in the light of the candles, and sometimes the roof of the gigantic cave they were in came so low above them they could reach up their hands and touch it.

"Yuggh!" whispered Miriam. "It's all covered in slime."

"Oooah yugghh" said Belle trying to wipe the gunge off her fingers.

"Well don't touch it then," said Sam as he took over the rowing with Miriam.

Slowly the cave got narrower and narrower. It was as if they were moving along an underground river.

"Stop," said Sam. "Take your oar out of the water."

Miriam did so and the boat floated forward.

"We don't have to row, the current's taking us."

"You mean I did all that rowing for nothing," said Alice rubbing her sore palms. "You might have told me."

"Be quiet, Alice," said Sam.

"Be quiet, Alice," she mimicked. "You'd make a good leader, Sam, I'll tell Fortuna."

"She already knows," said Sam.

"Yes, I suppose she does," said Alice. And privately she admitted to herself that if anybody would have made a good leader of Thistown it would have been Sam. And perhaps Fortuna really did know it.

She remained quiet as the boat slid forward over the dark water. They were by now only lighting one candle at a time so as to preserve their stock, but its single flame seemed more than enough. All they could see was the narrowing waterway and the black rocks around them. They began to lie back, letting the boat take them where it would. They shared some of the food that Belle had brought from the cave as they drifted further and further into the underground. They'd been going for hours and hours and there was no sign of the river ending, or of where it was going to take them. Slowly they all drifted off to sleep and the candle finally flickered and died as they glided slowly through the darkness.

It was then that the whispers started.

Alice woke and at first thought it was someone in the boat. She raised her head. "Who was that?"

They were slowly moving forward through the pitch black. Suddenly there was a long low moan.

"Who is it?" she asked again, "Would you mind stopping it, please? It's scary enough as it is."

"I wasn't me," said Sam, waking up himself.

"And it's not me, said Belle, scrambling up from where she'd been sleeping in the bottom of the boat.

"Nor me," said Jonny. "Light a candle"

Sam fumbled for the matches as the others woke up.

"What is it?" asked Miriam, as the moans and groans got louder around them.

Sam lit a candle and they looked around. It was exactly the same as it had been before they'd fallen asleep. Just the black, black river slowly gliding forward beneath the low slimy rock above. It was as if they hadn't moved. Except for the moans.

Miriam was immediately frightened, "What is it?" She peered into the darkness.

Then the whisperings started again, slithery sounds that seemed to slide from rock to rock, and more moans, and then a louder groan.

"It sounds like people in terrible pain," whispered Miriam.

"It's getting louder." said Jonny.

"What's that?" asked Alice. She'd heard a low, deep, thump. "There it is again."

The thumping sound continued like the slow beat of a huge drum.

"It's like a heartbeat," said Belle.

"Light some more candles," said Sam. "Perhaps we can see what it is."

They each lit a candle and held it up into the darkness, but all they could see was more rock and the river.

"There's nothing there," said Sam.

The low beat continued and the moans became even louder.

"I don't like it!" shouted Miriam.

Belle joined her, "Stop it! Stop it!"

"It's alright, it's alright!" Sam held her hand. "Whoever they are, they don't seem to be doing anything to us." He said.

"It's like we're going through a big stomach," said Alice, "and it's grumbling."

"And we've been eaten, you mean?" said Miriam, panicking again.

"Ssshh," said Sam. "It's not doing us any harm."

"It's the spirit of the Underworld," said Miriam, her eyes open wide. "Maybe it's where the No-Life Men go to?" said Alice suddenly. "I mean maybe it's where the life goes to after it's left them?"

"Why should it come here?" whispered Miriam.

"Well it's got to go somewhere," said Alice.

"Hey! Who are you!" Jonny shouted out.

But there was no answer except his echo and then more horrible gravelly groaning and moaning, and the low, regular thump.

"Perhaps it's just the sound of the rocks," said Sam.

Shouting out had made them feel better. It seemed that the sounds weren't going to do any harm to them. They slowly lay back in the boat.

"It's quite peaceful really," said Alice, "This rock talk."

No-one said anything else and they let the whispers slide over them as they moved forward. The low beat was quite calming, and one by one they felt their eyes closing and they fell asleep again.

THE SUN CONE

They were woken by a sudden sharp crack and jolt. Alice slipped off her seat and knocked Sam forward.

"What was that?" shrieked Belle.

"We must have hit something," said Jonny.

"Find the candles," said Sam.

Miriam struck a match and lit a candle.

"What's that?" Belle was staring up ahead of them at what seemed like a high wall of solid rock. More candles were lit and they peered from left to right, up and down. Just rock, huge ancient rock blocking their way.

"The moaning's stopped," said Miriam.

They looked around in the eerie silence.

"And the river's stopped," said Jonny, looking down at the water.

"A river can't just stop," said Sam. "It must flow somewhere."

"It's very shallow here," said Jonny leaning out of the back of boat, "I can touch the bottom."

"There!" said Alice. She was pointing towards a small hole in the bottom of the wall." The water's flowing through there."

"I'm going to have a look," said Sam.

He quickly took his shoes and socks off and lowered himself from the boat. He was surprised to see that the water only came up to his ankles, although it was still flowing quite quickly into the hole.

"There must have been other outlets for the water along the way that we didn't see," he said, as he made his way carefully towards the hole.

He crouched down and looked in. "It's a tunnel," he said. "Like the one we went through to get to the goldmine." He lowered himself even further. "And light! I can see light at the other end!"

Alice jumped out of the boat. In her excitement she forgot to take her shoes off. She slushed through the water to Sam and peered through the tunnel.

"It's not very long," she said. "I'm going through."

Sam said, "Alice be..."

".....careful," she finished it for him, but before he could stop her, she'd dropped to her knees in the water and started to crawl through the tunnel.

"It's getting even lighter!" she shouted from within it.

"I'm going too," yelled Belle.

"Wait a minute!" said Sam.

"Me too!" said Jonny.

And before Sam could do much about it, they were all in the water and heading for the tunnel.

"The boat!" yelled Sam, and he waded quickly back to tie it to a rock. By the time he'd done so, they'd all gone through and there was silence. He walked over to the hole, carefully lowered himself and began to crawl through.

The light became stronger and stronger as if it was drawing him towards it. There was no sound at all from ahead. His heart began to beat faster. What had happened to the others? He was nearing the end of the tunnel, and he felt a strange force as if it was pulling him on. He couldn't help himself and began to go quicker. And quicker. And suddenly he was out the other end.

What he saw amazed him as much as it had amazed the others. He was in a vast, high cavern and in the middle was a perfect cone of light coming from somewhere above them. It was so bright and clearly shaped that it looked solid like a pillar of gold that tapered upward. The others were silhouetted against it as Sam moved slowly forward. When he reached them he could see they were all smiling.

"I feel..." said Alice. She stopped and smiled.

"So do I...." said Miriam, beginning to giggle.

"I feel so happy!" Belle suddenly began to clap and jump in the air.

Sam looked up. The cone was making a perfect circle in the middle of the floor. "It's coming through a hole in the roof of the cave. It must be sunlight that's managed to wind itself down from up above."

"But doesn't it make you feel good?" asked Miriam.

"Yes," said Sam. He'd never felt happier in his life.

"Why does it do that?" asked Jonny.

"I don't know," said Sam. "We must be under the cornfields by now, so it's coming from there."

"I'm going into it," said Alice.

"Into the cone?" said Miriam, her eyes shining.

"Why not?" said Alice.

"Wait a minute...." said Sam.

But it was too late. Alice had stepped into the cone. They gasped in amazement. As soon as she'd entered the light, she'd completely vanished!

"Where's she gone?" said Belle looking round.

"She's disappeared," said Jonny.

"Alice!" Sam shouted. "Alice!"

There was no reply.

"It's alright," said Miriam. "I don't think any harm could come to her in there."

"How do you know?" asked Sam looking concerned.

"Because I feel so happy," said Miriam. "Something that does that couldn't harm anything."

And as if to prove her right, Alice stepped back out of the cone.

"What is it?" they all asked at once.

Alice stared at them, her eyes wide in excitement, "It's....it's....it's just brilliant," she could hardly keep the smile off her face. "I could see you all out here, but I couldn't hear you. I wanted to stay in there forever!"

"I'm going in," said Miriam.

"And you, Sam," said Alice.

"Alright," said Sam and he stepped into the cone and disappeared. Miriam followed and she disappeared too. And then Sam came out with the broadest grin on his face. And then Belle jumped in, and then Jonny. They all disappeared as they went in, and then re-appeared as they came out. It was like the best time of their lives. Rasper, Fortuna and Thistown were all forgotten as they darted in and out of the cone, laughing, dancing, jumping, disappearing and re-appearing.

"I feel like I'm floating in the air!" shouted Belle stepping out and then jumping back in.

"It's like you don't weigh anything when you're inside!" said Alice coming out.

"I couldn't feel my feet touching the ground," laughed Jonny.

"It's perfect. Just perfect," said Sam looking up at the shining cone. He walked round and round it. It never seemed to waver or change. It was just there, as if it had been there forever. "It's perfection."

"There's no way out," said Alice suddenly. He was looking up at the cavern on the other side of the cone. "There's no tunnel, or hole or anything."

"The river must have gone further underground," said Sam looking around for more water.

"What do we do now?" asked Jonny.

"I could stay here forever." said Belle.

"We hardly have any food," said Sam. "And we can't go on any further."

They were silent as they looked up at the giant cone.

"It's so beautiful," said Alice.

"I wish we could take it with us," said Sam.

"I think we can," said Alice thoughtfully.

"What do you mean?" asked Sam

"Well..." said Alice slowly, "I think the first thing we have to do is go back to Thistown."

"Go back to Thistown!" Belle looked very scared.

"They'll arrest us!" said Miriam.

"And put us in the basement!" said Belle.

Alice looked round at their frightened faces, "Yes, they'll do all of that," she said.

"Tell us Alice," said Sam.

"Well," she said, "I think we've found out something, and..." she beamed. "It's so simple!"

And then she explained. And what she said made Sam understand many things.

"All we have to do now, is be very, very brave." said Alice.

THE BASEMENT

"Get in there! Go on, move!" X Ray's harsh voice echoed along the corridor as Baz Brick and the guards dragged Alice, Sam and Belle down to the Town Hall basement. There was no light and all they could see were glimpses of harsh walls as they flashed by in the light of the Guard's torches.

"Alright, calm down X Ray." said Sam as he was pushed in the back.

"X! You call me X!" He produced a huge bunch of keys and unlocked a heavy iron door. "You won't be getting out again in a hurry," he leered. "Chain them to the wall."

"No!" screamed Belle as she struggled against Brick.

"You don't have to push!" Alice yelled angrily to X who had shoved her.

X grabbed her and pulled her face close to his. "Anymore out of you..."

"Your breath smells." said Alice defiantly

X raised his torch to hit her.

"Leave her alone'" yelled Sam.

"If she don't shut..." X shouted.

"And if you don't shut-up, you'll give us all a headache." This was Jack Juniper, Fortuna's favourite, who was leaning against the doorway, resplendent in his dark red uniform. "Hurry up and chain them to the wall. It stinks down here."

"Yeah, leave them to the rats." X leered as the guards took them, one by one and manacled them to heavy chains that were attached to huge iron rings in the wall.

"Mr Pen!" Alice had seen the old man first. He was lying on a piece of sacking in the darkness of the far corner. "Mr Pen, have they chained you too?"

"My dear, oh my dear, is it you?" He slowly sat up. "I heard you. I thought I was dreaming."

Alice erupted in fury at Jack. "Why is he here? He hasn't done anything! "

Jack smiled, "He was a friend of yours, and any friend of yours is an enemy of Her Highness."

"Her Highness!" Alice couldn't believe it. "You don't mean Fortuna?"

"Who else?" leered Jack.

"Highness!" Alice exploded, "Higher than what?"

"You for a start."

"And her great Highness locks up people who've done nothing all their lives except write a newspaper!"

X sniggered, "You got it. Now shut up or you'll *die*."

"*Die?*" said Sam, "What's *die?*"

"*Die!*" X roared with laughter in delight at his new word.

"*Dead*, don't you get it?" said Jack scornfully, "The No-Life Man is a *dead* man because he as no life. And as you get to be *dead*, you *die!* Get it?"

"What are you talking about," asked Sam.

"And we thought you were so intelligent," said Jack. "It's Fortuna language, you idiot. No-Life is called *dead*, and that's that."

"She's even telling you how to talk now?" sneered Alice.

"Shut-up, or you'll get this!" X suddenly smashed his torch into the wall above Alice's head, showering her with bits of broken glass. "Now you be careful, or we'll *kill* you, and that's another new word, and you can work out what that means yourself."

"All locked," said Brick, as he put the bunch of keys back on his belt.

"Enjoy yourselves," said X leaving.

"You were with us once, Jack," said Sam quietly.

"See you," grinned Jack. "I think I'll go and have dinner." He went out after X who turned and locked the door behind them.

"They're going to starve us, aren't they?" said Belle close to tears.

"We've got to be brave, Belle, remember?"

"Yes, Alice," snuffled Belle.

"Alice," Pen spoke from the darkness. "How many of you are there?"

"Me, Sam and Belle," she replied. "They've taken Jonny and Miriam to another basement."

"We didn't think it would be as bad as this," said Sam.

Aaaaaghh!" screamed Belle. "What is it? Something touched my foot!"

It's the rats," said Pen "Don't worry, they're harmless enough."

"It's alright, I'm brave," said Belle curling back against the wall, terrified.

"Tell me what happened to you?" asked Pen gently. "I don't think I have too long, you see?" he added weakly.

"Too long, what do you mean?" asked Alice in shock.

"Since you left, many people have *died* as they call it. Especially the old, my dear. We seem prone to it. They don't throw us in the corn if we are *dead*, because we just lie there and stink." he chuckled, "which serves them right, if you ask me." They put us in holes in the earth and cover us with stones. They call them *graves*. I don't think it will be too long before I...."

"No, Mr Pen! You mustn't say it!" Alice couldn't bear the thought of being without old Mr Pen."

"Tell me what happened," he said quietly, "You're the only thing that's left in Thistown that's any good."

BACK TO THISTOWN

"The return journey was much worse," said Alice. "We were rowing against the river current and sometimes we seemed to row for ages and get nowhere at all. And there was even one time when we seemed to slip back all the time, no matter how hard we rowed."

"And the moaning voices were much louder on the way back." said Belle.

"Or that's what they seemed anyway," said Sam. "I think it was because we were tired and just more frightened."

"And we were so hungry," said Alice. "There hadn't been much food in the cave in the first place and we'd eaten most of that by the time we'd got to the sun cone. And so coming back was a nightmare. Moany voices, and no food, and the river. But it was even worse when we got back to Thistown. We didn't make any secret of it, and just used the lift which the Fortunate Guard must have unblocked, and came straight up. They must have seen the big wheel turn, because as soon as we got to the top, there was X Ray with his gang of Fortunates in black uniforms."

"Everybody seems to be a Fortunate now," said Belle sadly.

"We saw hundreds of them in pink or black uniforms as they brought us back across the Green," said Alice.

"They're even building a statue of Fortuna there," said Sam. "It's huge. Vincente's doing it. When we were taken past him, I yelled out, but he just turned away."

"Even Rasper didn't dare to have a statue of himself." said Alice.

"He was too ugly!" said Belle.

"And so's Fortuna!" said Alice angrily, "There are pictures and posters of her everywhere. 'The Truly Great Ear,' and 'Fortuna the Saviour.' and others that say, 'Down with the Enemy!' I didn't get that. Who's the enemy?"

"That's what I asked," said Pen, "and that's why they threw me in here."

"Just for asking a question?" said Belle.

"This town is very different now," said Pen.

"But who is this enemy?" asked Sam.

"Fortuna has listened over the cornfields and says she's heard that we have enemies on the other side who will attack us unless we have an *army*." said Pen.

"An *army?*" asked Alice.

"It's another Fortuna word," said Pen. "It means a lot of *soldiers* who are all Fortunates dressed in green uniforms and march up and down. Apparently they will protect us against this enemy that could come at any time from over the Cornfields."

"Is this true?" asked Belle with her eyes wide.

"Of course it isn't," said Pen. "She can't see over the cornfields or listen over them any more than anyone else can. It's nonsense!" The old man seemed very angry. "The truth is," he said, "that the *soldiers* aren't really there to protect Thistown, they are there to protect Fortuna."

"And X," said Sam, "and Jack."

"And all her other friends..." said Alice.

"I think Fortuna will be the leader forever," said Pen sadly. "She's certainly clever enough."

At this the door suddenly opened again and X walked back in with Brick and several Guards behind him. Their lanterns lit up the basement as X stood arrogantly in front of them. He opened a cardboard file and read out.

"Alice Bright, Samson Stead, Bellina Fellows, you are charged with being enemies of Thistown. You will be tried in front of Her Highest Highness the Great Ear Fortuna in the Great Hall Palace tomorrow at noon."

And he snapped the file shut. "And that," he leered, "will be the end of you."

"And me too," said Pen with tears in his eyes, "If you are going to try them, try me too. I am with them!"

"You are an old fool." sneered X. "Her Highest Highness isn't interested in you. Go home."

"No!.." Pen protested.

"Get rid of him!"

Brick quickly unlocked Pen's chains and the Guards began to drag him out of the basement.

"Goodbye, Alice. Goodbye Sam. I shall always be with you." the old man shouted as they pulled him away.

"Goodbye, Mr Pen, I'll always love....." Alice began, but her old friend was already gone. She looked up at X and spat, "I feel sorry for you!"

X laughed and walked out of the basement as Brick slammed the door behind him.

"What are they going to do with us?" wailed Belle.

"They're going to do what we want them to do," said Alice. "They're going to take us to their court and try us."

THE TOWN THAT WAS

The first people they saw the next morning as Brick and his Guards led them out of the basement were Jonny and Miriam. They too looked pale and shaken.

"Are they taking you to the Great Hall as well?" asked Sam.

"I've never been an enemy of Thistown!" Jonny yelled. "And I never will be!"

"Shut up and stand still!" shouted Brick. "Chain them!"

The five of them were manacled together with chains round their wrists and ankles.

"Now take them out!"

They were pulled out through the great doors of the Town Hall and on to the steps. To their surprise there was a huge crowd of uniformed Fortunates spread out on the Green waiting for them. They immediately began to hiss and jeer.

"Enemies!"

"Throw them into the corn!"

Belle was frightened and she tried to hide behind Sam as they were all led forward. Miriam's usually beautiful golden face was white with fear as Brick pulled roughly on the chains holding them all. They were led towards an old and battered donkey cart that was fitted with what looked like an enormous wooden cage.

"Up there! Get up!" yelled Brick as he pushed them hard up into the cart.

Alice fell as she tried to mount the rickety wooden steps and Jonny couldn't help but fall on top of her.

"Get into the cart!" screamed Brick as he brought down his huge wooden club down on Jonny's back. Jonny cried out in pain. "Keep your mouth shut!" roared Brick as the crowd whistled and booed.

A driver got up in front and whipped the donkeys forward. Belle had often given these animals apples or carrots, but now they were carrying her to her trial.

"Hup! Hup!" the driver yelled as he cracked his whip in the air, the donkeys strained forward and the wheels of the cart started to turn.

Alice pulled herself up to look through the bars at the angry faces of the crowd. "They hate us." she said, "Why do they hate us?"

"Because of Fortuna," said Sam. "They'll do anything she says." He ducked as someone threw a rotten tomato at them.

That was the beginning of a hail of decaying vegetables thrown by the mob. They showered down on the cart. and covered them in putrid, stinking fruit, meat and anything else rotten the Fortunates could lay their hands on.

Jonny quickly got his own back by picking up an old apple and stuffing in his mouth. "It's the only way I'm ever going to get anything to eat!" he yelled, and his cheek cheered them all up.

"Stand up," said Sam. "Let them say and throw whatever they like."

And so they stood still and silent and let the crowd scream their worst as they passed beneath Vincente's statue of Fortuna in the middle of the Green. It was so vast it stood even higher than the Town Hall. The statue had been made of a pale pink stone and was so grotesque that even Alice was lost for words. Fortuna was looking sternly down Avenue A towards the Great Hall. One hand pointed towards the cornfields as if she was the ruler of them, and in the other stood a huge carving of an Ear as if it was growing out of her palm. Even the ear was bigger than Belle.

But then Alice realised that there was something about her head that wasn't quite right. She stared up as they passed underneath it and she realised that it was Fortuna's ears! The Great Ear's statue revealed that she had the tiniest ears that anyone had ever seen! Had Vincente had the last laugh? He wasn't there to say, but Alice suspected that he had. The cart came to a halt beneath the statue. And all the Guards raised their hands in the now familiar ear-cupping salute.

"You salute too!" Brick roared at them through the bars of the cage.

But they didn't move. All five of them stood still as the giant shadow of the statue fell over them.

"Salute!" the Brick shouted again.

Alice turned her head and said simply. "Salute what? I don't see anything except a lump of pink stone. With tiny ears. Why should I salute that?"

Brick didn't want the crowd to hear her. He snarled, "You'll pay for that, Alice Bright! Take them away!"

And the driver whipped the donkeys once more. And they passed across the rest of the Green through the still jeering crowd

"Look!" said Miriam pointing forward.

Avenue A was packed. It seemed as if the whole town had turned out to see them being taken to the Great Hall for the trial. The Fortunate Guard lined the Avenue with the silver buttons on their black uniforms polished to shine brightly in the mid morning sun. They pushed the crowd back against the buildings on either side. It was almost festive. Many of the people waved Fortuna flags or carried big placards with her stern, beautiful face bobbing up and down as her picture was carried through the throng. There were stalls, food sellers and even the Town Band which fell in behind the cart,

Sam moved his arm with difficulty to adjust his glasses. He was stunned by the size of the crowd.

"Thistown forever! The real Thistown! The Town you forgot!" Jonny suddenly yelled.

Brick who was running beside the cage poked his stick through the bars and caught Jonny in the stomach. "I told you! Keep your mouth shut!"

Jonny refused to cry out despite the pain. "You'll never beat it out of me, however hard you try!" he shouted. " Old Thistown for ever!"

As the cart made its way down the Avenue they could see that there were less Fortunate uniforms amongst the crowd. Perhaps all of Fortuna's followers had been told to assemble on the Green and there weren't enough of them to line the Avenue as well. And slowly a strange thing happened. The jeering began to stop. As soon as the crowd saw the dignified faces of the chained prisoners in the cart they went quiet. It was as if they could see the old Thistown and all it stood for mirrored in the eyes and bearing of these they were accusing. Several turned away in disgust at themselves. Most just looked down in shame. There were even a few tears, and at least one shout in the silence. "Sorry!"

For a while the cart was pulled forward in silence.

"What's that I can hear?" said Jonny turning back towards the Green.

"It's the sound of saws," said Sam.

"What are they sawing?" asked Alice.

No-one knew. The cage continued to rock backwards and forwards. They did their best to remain on their feet, looking only ahead. Many of the crowd began to disperse as the cage passed. Soon the only sound was the sound of sawing wood behind them and the band playing, but even they stopped as the cart passed into the huge walled yard of the Great Hall. Then something else began. It was the low sound of beating drums.

"Listen to that," whispered Miriam with huge frightened eyes.

The drums were like a huge heartbeat coming from deep within Thistown.

"It's like the beating underground," said Miriam.

"No, this is Fortuna," said Sam. "She's trying to show us her power."

"It's like she's beating out our last hours," said Jonny, looking down at the guards who were surrounding the cart.

THE FIVE ON TRIAL

"Get down!" Yelled Brick.

They were forced down from the cart and led into the Great Hall itself. Everyone inside was in a uniform of some kind, mostly pink, many black, and others red and orange, each depicting which part they played in the new order of Fortuna.

On the raised platform in front of the great window that looked out over the golden corn were two of those who'd once met in Old Pen's printing works to organise the Great Games that would bring down Rasper. Green Runner, and Charcoal Cheryl looked down on them. Rasper was forgotten. Having defeated him they were all for Fortuna.

They stared with hard faces as the five were brought in and pushed roughly into a pen that had been erected in the middle of the huge space. They knew that there would be no mercy, but still they stared defiantly at their former friends. They knew they were in the right too. And probably these unfortunate Fortunates knew it too. By following Fortuna they had betrayed Thistown and themselves. How could they not know it?

The drumming got louder, and then louder, until it was impossible to hear anything else, and then suddenly it stopped, to be replaced by a single trumpet playing the highest most piercing note ever heard. Everyone stood and the silver doors at the back of the hall opened. Tess the Dress came through in a deep maroon robe with jewels at her throat. After her came X in his jet black jacket. His highly polished boots shone as brilliantly as the silver buttons on his tunic. Then came Jack Juniper in his dark red uniform. They came to the front of the platform and stood looking contemptuously down on the five.

There was a silence. Everyone waited. Then the trumpeter played another three notes each higher than the one before and suddenly everyone in the hall bowed low as Fortuna swept in. Her black hair was pulled away from her face and rose in gleaming coils behind her head. Her pale yellow skin shone, and her diamond eyes flashed above rosebud lips and the deepest pink, flowing, glistening silk gown. She was so beautiful that the crowd gasped.

"The Great Ear!" shouted X.

"Her Highness!!" yelled Jack Juniper.

"The Queen of the Corn!!" roared the Fortunate Guard as one.

The five in the pen still hadn't moved. The drums started beating again, low under the measured footsteps of Fortuna as she slowly moved towards the great golden chair in the centre of the platform. She sat and looked round the silent hall. Finally her gaze settled on the five.

"Well," she purred, "I am sorry to see you here."

"Get on with it, Fortuna," said Alice defiantly. "I can remember you falling out of a tree on the Green!"

"Shut-up!" snapped Jack.

"Let her. Let her." Fortuna fanned herself with a jewelled fan. "She hasn't got long." She smiled sweetly.

"You still know us, whatever you pretend." said Alice proudly from behind the bars.

The drums stopped suddenly as Fortuna turned away from them and nodded towards Jack

He jumped up and bowed to her, "Your Highness." Then he turned to the five and looking down his nose, said, "You are traitors. You have betrayed Thistown. You are our enemies. Before Her Highness delivers her judgement, she has generously allowed you the opportunity to speak. What do you want to say?"

"So this is not a trial, you've already decided what's going to happen to us," Alice shouted into the bleakness of the Great Hall, never wavering in her stare at Fortuna, who didn't look back.

"We all know what you did." X said.

"What exactly did we do?"

"You accused our Great Leader or favouritism, of lying and of murder!" said Jack pointing his finger. "In front of the Town Assembly. It's a matter of public record!"

"Why shouldn't we accuse her?" Alice shouted back. "Who does she think she is?"

There was a stunned silence in the Hall at this impertinence.

"I shall ignore that," said Fortuna softly. She nodded at Jack who continued.

"You resisted arrest by the Fortunate Guard and fled to the goldmine!"

"What's wrong with going down a mine?" yelled Jonny defiantly. "The first time we went down you were with us!"

"That was in the great revolution against Rasper!" said Jack. "The Gold Mine is now Town Property."

"The Town's property belongs to all of us," said Sam quietly.

"The Town's property is the property of our leader!" shouted Tess angrily.

Jack went on, "You have also conspired to bring down the Great Ear! These are the charges and you are guilty."

"Who says so?" asked Alice.

"We do!!" The Fortunates on the platform all shouted as one.

"So now you have wasted our time with your pointless interruptions," said Jack, "I'll ask you once again if you have anything to say."

Alice turned to Sam who nodded. He came slowly to the front of the cage. He looked ahead at all his old friends who were now ranged against him. Then he looked up. High in the hall sitting alone in the furthest balcony was Old Pen, who seemed to be nodding in encouragement. The old man's smile gave Sam heart.

"Yes, I have something to say," his voice rang out through the hall, "We are not enemies. All of us were altogether once when we defeated Rasper. All of us, including you, Fortuna."

X leapt to his feet. "Her Highness! You will call her Your...."

"I will call her Fortuna!" Sam interrupted him. "She is exactly the same as the rest of us."

The Hall was immediately filled with angry cries and shouts. It looked as though the Fortunate Guard were going to attack the five there and then.

"We have decided what we will do," said Sam ignoring the pandemonium. "We didn't have to come back here to you."

"Oh yes, you were going to come up from the mine and walk out across the corn, were you? " said X sarcastically.

There was a roar of laughter which was immediately silence by the tiniest movement of Fortuna's hand. She said with a sweet smile. "If you knew what you were going to do and you didn't have to come back, why did you?"

"Because we wanted to talk to you first," said Sam. "To try and persuade you that you were wrong." He turned to the crowd, "we wanted you to know that what is happening now is the end of Thistown."

"Is that a threat?" asked X nastily.

"No," said Sam, "It's not us who will destroy Thistown, it's you."

"I'm getting bored," said Fortuna.

" I will tell you only what we came to say, "said Sam. He waited until there was absolute silence and then went on, "You do not need a Great Ear to listen out for you. If we listened to ourselves we would know we didn't need guards, or Great Halls, or armies, or leaders of any kind. All those things have made us unhappy."

"That's rubbish, we're happy!" Several of the Fortunates shouted out.

"I know you all." said Sam, "You Ray, and Jack, and Tessa. And you Fortuna. We know what you are going to do to us."

Oh do you?" sneered Jack.

Sam ignored him. He wanted to make them think.

"After this, when you go home..."

"When we go home, yes, yes, yes...to our beautiful homes..." X-Ray was looking at the ceiling.

"When you go home," Sam went on, "think of what it used to be like in Thistown when none of us grew older and when there were no No-Life People, or *dead* people."

Jack was smirking and X-Ray was beginning to giggle, but Sam could see that others in the great hall were silent and looking down at the floor..

Alice could see that there were tears in Sam's eyes as he said quietly. "Just ask yourselves, which was better. Which do you prefer? Then or Now?" He looked round. "That's all I came to say" And he sat down.

There was no more laughter. Alice could see that many people had listened to Sam carefully and knew exactly which they preferred. They preferred Thistown as it used to be. But no-one spoke. There was just a horrible silence. Everyone was to scared of Fortuna and her guards.

"Well, how fascinating," said Fortuna into the silence. "No-one speaks, so no-one seems to agree with you. It seems we prefer things the way they are."

The Fortunates all stood and applauded, but many were looking down at the ground.

"I don't know what this mysterious thing is you've decided to do." Fortuna said.

"You'll help us do it," Alice said quietly.

"There's only one thing I'll do for you!" Fortuna suddenly shouted, her patience at an end. "And whatever secret you think you have, it won't do you any good! You are going to the cornfields! And you are going now! The preparations are already under way!" She stood up. "Take them out!" she shouted.

The drums started to beat louder.

"Throw them into the corn!"

WAITING FOR THE CORN

The five of them sat locked in a small room under the Great Hall. They were still chained together, but compared to the Town Hall it was an improvement. There were no rats, the light was on and someone had even given them a bowl of rotten fruit to eat.

Jonny chewed a sour pear with a grimace. But no-one else was hungry. They could still hear the drums beating softly outside.

"Are you sure you're right about the corn, Alice?" said Miriam getting more terrified by the second.

"As sure as I can be," said Alice, although she was beginning to sound a bit doubtful herself.

"But what if we just disappear and never come back!" Belle was beginning to panic. "No-one's ever come back from the corn."

"I don't want to be in Thistown anyway," said Jonny spitting out the brown core of his pear.

"We don't know what is going to happen, that's the truth." said Miriam miserably. "We may get *dead*."

"Believe," said Alice, "just believe."

No-one knew what else to say.

"Listen!" said Jonny, standing up.

"I don't want to!" cried Miriam covering her ears. "I hate those drums!"

"No, not the drums," said Jonny pulling himself up closer to a window high in the wall. "It's the sound of sawing again. Can you hear it? Someone's sawing something. What do you think it is, Sam?"

Sam was sitting hunched in a corner, deep in thought. "I don't know," he said. "They're probably building another statue of Fortuna."

"I hate her! I hate her!" Belle burst out.

Suddenly the door was thrown open.

"Samson Stead!" X strode into the room with two guards. "Unlock his chains."

"Why?" asked Sam.

"Shut-up! You've been granted an audience with the Her Highness."

"Fortuna?"

X tugged at the chain wrenching Sam's arm. "You call her that again and I'll....I'll..."

"Throw him in the corn?" asked Alice, her eyes wide. "I think Fortuna's already decided that, hasn't she?"

X pushed his face close to hers, "Say what you like. Soon you'll be *dead*."

The chains fell from Sam's wrists. "Take him out."

"Sam," said Miriam as he was pushed to the door, "Can you ask...I mean....if there's any way... that her Great Highness could.....I mean." she looked at Sam with her huge frightened, grey eyes. "I'm scared of the corn!" And she suddenly burst into tears.

Before Sam could reply Alice stood up. "Don't Sam! Don't tell Fortuna anything."

Sam was pulled away by the guards. The last thing he heard before the door was slammed shut was Alice pleading, "Don't! Don't tell her!"

He was pushed and prodded down a hallway and then up a long flight of stairs. All the time he was thinking and thinking. Alice knew what Fortuna was going to ask him, and so did he, but he had no idea of how he was going to answer her. He was then taken along what seemed like a never-ending corridor past more guards and finally up another shorter set of steps. He was stopped before a door made of solid gold.

HER HIGHEST HIGHNESS

After a second the golden door was opened by Tess. She looked out at Sam with contempt. "Bring him in." The Guards began to move forward. "Not you! You don't come into Her Highness' chamber! You." She'd said the last to X who roughly pushed Sam forward into the room and closed the door behind them.

Sam stumbled forward and stopped. He couldn't believe his eyes. The entire room, walls, doors and furniture was made of gold. And through the gold framed windows was the enormous expanse of the cornfields stretching to the horizon, and they were golden yellow too. But perhaps the most amazing sight was Fortuna herself. She was sitting in front of a vast mirror. Her dress was made of gold thread and two maids were painting her face. Huge red flames shot out of her green eyes and frightening orange stripes ran down the sides her cheeks. Her small lips were painted gold.

Jack Juniper stood by her as usual, his red uniform gleaming in the reflected golden light.

"Ah Sam," Fortuna hardly bothered to look at him, being too intent on her own image in the mirror. "Sit down."

Jack pushed a small stool into the back of Sam's legs and he fell rather than sat on it. He regained his balance and waited. Fortuna seemed to be ignoring him. She was concentrating on her face.

"Finally she said, "How does it feel to be going into the corn?"

Sam said nothing.

There was another long silence as Fortuna slowly painted around her eyes. "As you once helped me get rid of Rasper, I'm going to give you one last chance." She paused and looked at Sam through the mirror. "Tell me what you've decided to do and I may save you from the corn."

This is the question that Sam had been dreading. Fortuna had turned back to the mirror. What was he to say to her? Should he tell her about the sun cone?

She turned towards him again. "I'm waiting."

He didn't know what to say. If he didn't tell her then no-one else in Thistown would ever know about what they'd discovered. He remembered when they'd got rid of Rasper and he'd said nothing even though he'd thought it was wrong. And look what happened then. Everything had got worse. So shouldn't he tell the truth now?

"Are you going to keep me waiting forever?"

But what would Fortuna do if he told her? She wouldn't tell the rest of the town, would she? Or would she? He thought of Alice shouting, "Don't tell her! But he knew he should tell. It was a discovery that everyone should know. He should have told them all at the trial. He knew that now.

"Don't you want to saved from the corn?" Fortuna purred.

And he suddenly blurted it out. "If you go into the corn you'll be alright."

"What do you mean, you'll be alright?"

Fortuna was looking at him as if he was stupid and that's exactly how he felt. He had to either tell her or not tell her. He couldn't just half do it.

He said, "We think, that if you go in the corn…you won't disappear forever."

Fortuna turned slowly and stared at him. He immediately wished he hadn't opened his mouth. If Fortuna believed him, she might decide to starve them all in the basement instead. And he would be responsible then for the *dead* of his friends.

"What?" said Fortuna smirking at Tess. "Are you saying that if you go in the corn, you'll be alright?"

It was too late to stop it now. Sam told her about the sun cone and the feeling of lightness and brilliance, and how they couldn't believe that any harm could ever come from such beauty, and as the sun came down from the corn above, they didn't believe that the corn could do them any harm either.

"The corn doesn't do us any harm?" said Fortuna.

"No," said Sam, "I don't believe it does."

"So it didn't take Rasper's leg then?"

"Well, yes it did that."

"And all those people who went into the corn and never came back, they're perfectly alright as well, are they?" Fortuna was beginning to smirk. "Well, perhaps I'd better go and listen to it and see if you're right," said Fortuna, and she got up, walked quickly over to the window and cupped her ear with her hand. "I don't hear anything at all, Sam."

"That's not surprising is it?" he said. "You never have."

"Shut-up!" Jack shouted.

"How dare you!" Fortuna snapped. "How dare..!" she stopped mid sentence. "Well, Sam, that's a very interesting theory, isn't it?" She began to smirk. "The corn doesn't do us any harm? And disappearing forever is good for you, is it?"

"I don't know for sure," said Sam. And he suddenly felt very worried about what he and Alice and the others were planning to do.

"You don't know. And where do you think we disappear too then?"

"I...I don't know that either"

"Oh he doesn't know that either!" Fortuna was now openly grinning at Tess and Jack.

"No, I don't know, but I don't think it's bad," said Sam nervously.

"He doesn't think it's bad!" Jack hooted.

"He's corngone!" gasped Tess.

"Corngone!" X laughed.

"It's perfectly alright to disappear!" Tess clapped her hands in delight.

"To nowhere in particular!" Jack was doubled up with laughter.

"Let him find out!" shrieked Fortuna. "I think we can help!"

As they laughed Sam watched the corn blowing lazily through the window. He thought of Run and the corn travellers; they'd gone into the corn and never been seen again, and nor had Rasper. So what would happen to them? He knew they'd never come back. But where would they go? *Dead?* Miles away over the corn he could see a tiny black cloud. He sat on the stool as the Fortunates laughed. He'd told them what he thought was the truth, but now he wasn't so sure it was.

THE EDGE

The little cloud Sam had seen through Fortuna's window came closer and closer until it covered the whole of Thistown and became the biggest cloud that they'd ever seen. It hovered low in the sky over the town, cutting out the last of the evening sun. Hundreds of people were hurrying down Avenue A to see the five traitors thrown from the Edge into the corn. Many of them were carrying flame torches against the dark.

The drums were beating louder and faster as the five were dragged out of the Great Hall and into the yard. Once again they were thrown into the wooden cage on the cart, and once again the driver cracked his whip and drove the huge donkeys forward, this time back out through the gates of the Great Hall.

Sam had told them how Fortuna had laughed when he'd told her what they'd discovered. Alice had been furious with him, but how could she be angry now? This was their last journey together ever in Thistown. Of all of them she had the strongest belief that everything would be alright, but as she looked out through the gates at the sombre, torch lit crowds that lined their route along the Edge, even she was beginning to have doubts. The cart moved forward again.

"What will they do to us?" Belle's face was wet with tears.

Miriam couldn't speak. Even Jonny had finally gone quiet and Sam could only hear his own heartbeat.

"Believe," said Alice, "Believe."

"Ahh!" screamed Miriam. "Look!"

"So that's what the sawing was." said Jonny going pale.

Ahead of them was one of the great oaks from the Green. It had been cut down and stripped of all its branches except for the first fork in the trunk. Then it had been planted back into the ground near the corn. Further along they could see another four oaks all standing along the Edge like giant letter Y's silhouetted against the darkening sky and the glimmering corn beyond. Each had a great fire burning beneath it. Huge ropes had been attached to the tops of the trees and hundreds of men were heaving to bend them back. The cart trundled closer, the crowd yelled and the men pulled on the ropes until the trees were bent back almost double with their trunks in the earth and their tops touching the ground behind. Men lashed them down to huge pegs and others came to tie huge leather pouches between the two branches of the Y.

Sam saw immediately what the Fortunates were going to do. Each of them would be put in a pouch, the ropes holding the top of the tree bent back to the ground would be cut, the tree would spring forward, springing whoever was in the pouch high into the air over the cornfields.

"They're like giant catapults!" he said, amazed. "They're going to fire us into the corn."

"I don't want to do it!" yelled Miriam as the drums beat louder.

The cart came to a halt by the fire at the first tree near the top of Avenue Y. The crowd pushed forward and suddenly there was a loud crack of thunder from the dark cloud above.

"No, not me!" Miriam hung on to the bars of the cage.

Suddenly there was a ear piercing blast of trumpets, and a cheer from the Fortunates among the crowd and along the Edge. The five turned back towards the Great Hall as Fortuna came out on to a high balcony. Huge lanterns hung behind her. She was dressed in the gold robe, there were red flashes painted on her face and gold stars on her forehead. She gleamed and glittered in the light from the fires and the lanterns. Behind her were Tess, Jack and X. The drums pounded louder and the Fortunates roared as Fortuna stepped forwards to a microphone and raised her golden arms high.

"My People!"

Her speech was interrupted by another huge clap of thunder and a streak of lightning, followed by a bang.

"Lightning strike!" someone shouted.

"It's a sign from over the corn!" Fortuna shouted into the microphone. "It's telling us to rid Thistown of these traitors forever!"

The Fortunates cheered and so did many others in the crowd.

"Let us begin!" she yelled. "The traitor, Jonny Ridge-wood!"

"No...no..." yelled Jonny. He didn't want to be first! He hardly had time to speak before two huge Fortunates came up into the cage and pulled him out.

"Leave him! Leave ..." Miriam tried to hold onto him.

"No, Miri. No." Sam had taken her arm. "We've done it now."

"And we have to be brave." smiled Alice, although her face was pale.

"That's right. We have to do it," said Jonny as the guards dragged him out of the cart. He was taken to the first tree. He looked back and tried to smile as they put him into the pouch, but his face was frozen with fear.

"Jonny Ridgewood! Let him eat corn!" Fortuna's voice boomed through the speakers.

"Let him eat corn!!" the crowd yelled as a Fortunate Guard took a burning torch from the fire and held it to the great rope holding the top of the tree to the ground. There was another great clap of thunder and more lightning. The rope burnt and finally snapped, releasing the top half of the huge oak. It sprang forward and Jonny was shot high into the air over the corn. His arms and legs were spread wide. He didn't scream, but the crowd did. They roared their approval as he landed in the corn. And he was gone.

Miriam had squeezed her eyes tight shut. She couldn't look. "Goodbye, Jonny."

"Something's been struck by lightning!" Someone yelled.

"Yeah, Jonny Ridgewood!" Someone else yelled back as the rest laughed and the cart trundled forward to the next tree.

"The Traitor, Belle Fellows!" Fortuna shouted into the microphone.

"Goodbye Sam, goodbye...." Belle wasn't allowed to finish as the powerful arms of the Fortunates lifted her small body and carried her to the pouch tied into the second tree.

"Goodbye Belle..." Sam began.

"We'll see you..." shouted Alice.

There was more thunder and lightning and another bang somewhere towards the centre of the town.

"Something else's been struck...." someone shouted.

"Drums! Drum louder!" Fortuna yelled into the microphone. She didn't want her big event ruined by a bit of lightning and a few tiny fires. "Belle Fellows! Let her eat corn!"

"Let her eat Corn!!" The crowd yelled as brave Belle, the youngest of the five who'd kept them all alive in the goldmine, was fired into the air. She let out a long high wail as she thrashed her arms and legs. Her tiny figure came down into the corn over two hundred yards from the Edge. And little Belle was gone.

No-one in the cart had dared to look except Alice.

"It's alright, I think it's alright," she said as she watched Belle disappear.

"How can you know!" screamed Miriam, as the great donkeys pulled the cart forward to the third tree.

"The sun cone!" shouted Alice, close to tears herself.

"The Traitor, Miriam Marjorami!" Fortuna's hated voice boomed from the speakers, and more Fortunates came up into the cage and grabbed Miriam.

"Remember the sun cone! We went in and we came...."

But Miriam was gone from the cage. She didn't struggle as they put her into the pouch. The last Thistown saw of her was her pale face illuminated by the burning torch as a Fortunate burnt the rope holding the top of the tree to the ground.

She flew through the air but didn't struggle against it as the others did. She just seemed to fly straight ahead.

"Whhooosshhh!" screamed the crowd.

And sweet Miriam with all her herbs and potions was gone.

"There's a fire! A fire in the Town Hall! The lightning's struck it!!" This time it was a Fortunate Guard who shouted it.

"Drum louder!" Fortuna ordered from the safety of the balcony.

"Look!" said Sam pointing towards the Green. "There are fires everywhere!" He could see that many in the crowd were beginning to feel frightened and some of them were running back towards the fires in the centre of the town. But most were too scared to move. They seemed to be hanging onto Fortuna's words for safety.

She shouted, "The traitor, Alice Bright!"

The cart moved forward towards the fourth tree, but then a strange thing happened The tree sprung up on its own with its pouch empty. Perhaps the rope holding it had broken or had been burnt through by a stray spark.

"The fifth tree! Take them both to the fifth tree!" This time it was X who had taken over the microphone and shouted into it.

The cart trundled on to the last tree with only Sam and Alice left. They could see that the fires in the town were burning even more wildly, and even more members of the crowd were running back into the town, but not the Fortunate Guard. They still lined the Edge and screamed their hatred as Sam and Alice passed them.

"Traitors! Into the corn!"

The cart stopped and like Jonny, Sam and Alice got down on their own.

"You can get into together!" Brick leered as he led them to the pouch. He'd obviously saved the last tree for himself. "And you can fly together!"

"Alice! Alice!" It was old Pen who was pushing himself through the crowd.

"Mr Pen!" Alice tried to get to him but was held back by the guard.

"Alice!" Pen held his hand out to her.

She tried to reach it. "We are right, Mr Pen! I know we are right! Throw yourself into the...." Alice shouted, but there was more thunder and her voice was drowned as she was pulled away from him and pushed towards the last pouch with Sam.

"The lightning's got the stables!"

"Who cares!" yelled someone else. It was as if they wanted Thistown to burn.

"The Traitor, Sam Stead and the Traitor, Alice Bright!" Fortuna shouted.

Suddenly there was a bright flash and a terrible explosion that shook the whole town. Lightning had hit the Great Ear on top of the Great Hall immediately above

Fortuna. The whole building was engulfed in flames. With the fire spreading and roaring behind her, Fortuna in her golden dress, shone as brightly as the sun. Jack and X tried to pull her from the balcony and to safety, but she hadn't finished her terrible work.

"Sam Stead and Alice Bright! I hate them! *Let them eat corn!!*"

This time nobody yelled. Perhaps too many of them had gone to try and put out the fires, or perhaps they were finally beginning to realise that it wasn't Sam who was corngone, it was Fortuna.

Only Brick cackled. He held his flaming torch down to the rope and said, "Bye bye."

THAT-TOWN

These were the last words Sam and Alice heard before the tree sprung and they were shot up into the air. As they flew through the darkness they could see that the lightning had set fire to the whole of Thistown and it was burning from the centre to the Edge. The yellow of the corn shimmered in the light of the fires. Their old town was burning up and soon would be gone.

Alice reached for Sam as they flew. She wanted him to believe too, and as she felt his hand in hers, she knew he did. And as they came down towards the corn she knew it was going to be like the sun cone. They were going to disappear and they were going to......

"Sam!" It was the last thing Alice said for quite a time as they plummeted down and down through the yellow corn. They felt it whip against their faces. They still held hands as they fell. And suddenly it was as if they were floating. There was no more corn. They'd come through it as Alice had always believed they would. They were floating in the light like the sun-cone. They were alright. They were just fine. The corn wasn't to *kill* them as X Ray thought, or to take the life from them as Fortuna imagined. The corn wasn't No-Life. It was New Life!

Alice smiled the most brilliant smile as she floated. She could see Sam smiling too. It was peaceful and quiet as they looked about them and saw that they were surrounded by stars. And below them they saw Jonny, and further down they could see the tiny shapes of Belle, and Miriam. They were all falling and falling, travelling millions of miles a second down through the universe. It was as if they were going in slow motion, falling slowly into a new beginning.

Sam and Alice caught up with the others and they all held hands, a circle of five friends, all feeling the intense happiness of the sun-cone as they descended through the stars. They watched in wonder as they passed a vast, bright planet to their left, and then another to their right. And more stars, thousands of stars, millions of stars, lighting their way as they slowly fell through the universe.

After what seemed like days and days of the most serene and beautiful and wondrous and joyous journey, Sam pointed down. Beneath them was a tiny dot. As they descended the dot slowly got bigger and bigger. At first it seemed as if half of it was bright blue and the other half dark. Then as they got closer they could see that the blue was speckled with swirly white, and then they saw it was green and brown too.

Slowly, slowly they came down until they were flying through cloud with mist on their faces. And then they had the most brilliant and dazzling sight of their lives. It was something that filled them with the utmost joy. They laughed and danced in the air in sheer delight as they descended with all their goodness and strange powers to their new home. Planet Earth.